VICTORIA - A CINCO DE MAYO BRIDE

MIMI MILAN

EATON HOUSE

International Bestselling Author

MIMI MILAN

Brides OF NOELLE
Love For All Seasons

Victoria

A Cinco De Mayo Bride

Victoria – A Cinco de Mayo Bride

© 2018 by Michele Claudio

Cover design by EDH Graphics

❦ Created with Vellum

What others are saying about Mimi Milan's books:

"*I thoroughly enjoyed* A Rebel in Jericho. *I felt that it was a great read. The plot was interesting and kept me turning the pages to find out what would happen next. The characters were well developed and interesting. I enjoyed the historical aspect and the description at the end of real events hinted at in the story. I like that the ending lends itself well to a sequel while effectively completing this story. I can't wait to read more by this author.*

I love that 20 percent of the sales from this book goes toward stop- ping human trafficking which is a bigger problem than we realize."

~ Carrie, Reader ~

"A Rebel in Jericho *has a little of everything for its readers to enjoy. Suspense, romance, deception, and the desire to survive. Catalina has an incredible strength within herself, while at the same time showing just how vulnerable she is. I was intrigued to find out what twist and turns would take place next with every page I turned. I look forward to continuing reading this series and what other adventures are to come.*"

~ Warrior Ground ~

"This novel [Twice Redeemed] *touches on human trafficking and tugs on the human heart. The author, Mimi Milan, is a master storyteller. She invites the reader into her fictional story world set in Mexico and drops them into the scene of action. The reader experiences the story as if they are an observer watching the story of Jericho unfold. As they turn each page, the readers become invested in the plot, grow fond of the good characters, want to silence the bad guys and care deeply about how the story ends.*

The author drives the characterization deep and paints a picture on every page. The descriptions of each setting are vivid and believable. The dialogue is engaging and fresh. The plot thickens with the turn of each page and the theme of God's grace moves forward this story of redemption.

I believe that this story is worth every bit of a five-star rating. It's worthy of winning a literary award."

~ Writer at Heart ~

"*I really enjoyed all three of the novellas in this series* (the Angel Paws Rescue series). *Each novella is surprisingly very different from the other, but each has a wounded veteran and an arts person as the hero and heroine with a pet/service animal adopted from Angel Paws Rescue. I recommend the series to anyone who enjoys clean, heart-warming contemporary romance."*

~ MH, Reader ~

To those who know the struggle...
You have always been beautiful and worthy,
and that is how you will win the battle ~
with exquisite merit.

ACKNOWLEDGMENTS

I know that the books I write are only considered "sweet," but it would be a complete fail on my part if I did not give thanks to the Creator. Without the blessings of imagination and gab, I wouldn't have any stories to tell. So, I remain eternally grateful to the Master Storyteller who designs each of us with a purpose. I'm glad my purpose is to write books!

A book cannot come together without a team, though. At the top of the team's list is Patricia Highton as she continues to work miracles via edits. I've scaled back considerably on the ellipses thanks to her. (Aren't you proud of me, Pat?)

To a handful of readers and writers who never fail me... Marianne, Tracy, Sarah, Sandy, Karen and too many more to list. I didn't ask permission to thank you in writing. That's why there's only first names. You know who you are, though, and you are much more than just Facebook or Twitter friends to me. I look forward to your posts and (for those of you who write) your books as well. If you didn't know, now you do—you are all my silent inspiration. Your kind words help me get through many days.

To the ladies of Pioneer Hearts "Accountability" group—

thank you for holding me accountable. With everything going on in my personal life, this book really struggled to make it to the finish line. The daily goal posts helped get it there.

To my husband, Guillermo, the battle has only just begun (again). It seems like we gain one step only to take three back, but that's okay. We do not fight alone. We have been graced with a beautiful community of caring souls, and that is why we will be victorious. Of course, the victory is the Lord's and no one can truly know what that means. We have to remember that He answers prayers, but sometimes the answer isn't what we expect. I hope that it is the same as my heart desires, but I also know that "the heart can be treacherous." Perhaps what He wants for us is better than what we've imagined for ourselves. Ah, well. Whatever it may be, I will have faith that all things work out for good in the end. I hope and pray in the meantime that you are doing well. The children and I look forward to the day when we will all be reunited once more. Until then, all my love and appreciation for the three small sugars who remain in my keep. They are the sweetest gifts I could have ever known.

CHAPTER 1

*oelle, Colorado*
April 7, 1877

SHE WAS GOING to get that building if it was the last thing she ever did!

Victoria Villanueva let out a little *humph!* as she slammed the door to the land office. She was too new in town to know all the residents, but already she could tell which ones she didn't care much for. Amongst them was Solomon Sharp. Unfortunately, the new agent for the railroad was also the land office manager... and he was apparently of the mind that women had better use for a husband than a prime parcel of real estate in the middle of town. With an attitude like that, she didn't know how the man had ever found a wife.

She sighed, deciding to be thankful that at least he allowed her to bid on the property. Now she only had to pray that no one came up with a price the man found more appealing.

Victoria walked back down the main street of Noelle, towards her cousin's restaurant, *Nacho's Tacos*. Ignacio and his wife, Josefina, had done a fine job with the place. They were more than eager to let her start up a *panandería* inside their restaurant, too. It was kind of them, but she wanted her own bakery—a little shop with an apartment up top. She would sell her sweets by day and fall asleep to fragrant flavors of vanilla spice at night. That was the secret ingredient to her prized tres leches cake. It was the one thing her mother had passed down before the Battle of...

No. She wasn't going to think of it again. A good fifteen years had passed since she lost most of her family to war. Thinking about them only served to make her feel like a lost eight-year-old child again, being shipped from one relative to another until finally making her way to America to be raised with Nacho and the rest of her cousins. They had been good to her, too. His own mother had taken Victoria under her wing and showed her how to cook. When she found the recipe for the tres leches cake buried in the bottom of her carpet bag with a lone family photo, the tía who had taken her in also showed Victoria how to put together her own recipe book. It looked very similar to the one the Villanueva matron constructed, but there were less savory meals and more sweet ones in Victoria's collection.

She smiled at the thought that now both collections safely resided in her cousin's kitchen at *Nacho's Tacos*. Together, they would take the town by storm!

Victoria paused at the building that held her interest most —the one that boasted a sign in the front window, "For sale." She caught sight of herself in the window. Save the fact that she was a little... fluffy... from taste testing her own wares, she was put together well. She wished she could blame the extra padding on height, but Josefina and she were of the same stature (save the little rolls Victoria carried in her midsection) and her new *prima* had a svelte figure that could rival any in *Harper's Bazaar*. She straightened up and ran one hand down her stomach before looking up. Fairer than the rest of her family, her features declared war with one another. Dull brown eyes with specks of green announced her French heritage, but their sharp almond shape denied the father who traversed Mexico long before Napoleon III had taken a liking to it. Further, her nose and mouth were generous like that of her Mexican mother. The hair could only be described as *canela*—a rich auburn hue much like the cinnamon sticks she grated to sprinkle in her coffee every morning. She didn't know where in the world she got the texture of her hair, though. Victoria reached up to once again tuck away a persistent curl that insisted on escaping the loose bun she wore. She looked over the reflection one last time.

Perhaps I should find a husband.

An irritated *tsk* escaped through her teeth and she walked on, crossing the street to the restaurant, musing all the while about how no man would care for a grown woman of twenty and four who looked as though she had already birthed her parcel of babies. At least, she was sure none of the men in Noelle would ever want *her*. All the eligible ones were spoken for. The rest... well... *most* of the others seemed to find comfort at the bottom of the bottle or in the arms of a soiled dove. She might not be of nobility—at least, she wasn't since her father cut off his family to marry a "savage" woman. Still, she didn't ever want a "better to be miserable than alone" prospect like a few of her friends back home suffered. No, that wouldn't do at all.

Victoria pushed open the door to the restaurant only to be welcomed by the hustle and bustle of a Monday morning work day.

"Good morning, *prima*." Nacho welcomed his cousin with

a wide grin that didn't quite reach his eyes. He quickly poured a cup of coffee for one patron and then returned his attention to her. "I didn't know you were going out this morning."

Victoria stifled a sigh, struggling to hide her irritation. This was another reason she needed to find her own place. Her cousin had the terrible tendency of constantly keeping account of her whereabouts. She didn't want or need him worrying about her—especially for something like going out in pursuit of her dreams.

"I didn't know I had to tell you when I was going out for a stroll," she snapped.

The remark held a bit more bite than she had intended it to. Nacho's expression fell flat.

"I'm sorry, Tori. After the problems Josefina encountered when she first arrived, I was only concerned for your safety."

Between the use of her childhood nickname and the genuine concern in his voice, she couldn't help but feel guilty. How could she be so rude after all his family had done for her?

"*Disculpa*, Nacho. Please, excuse me. Perhaps I should have eaten one of those *conchas* I made earlier."

"You didn't eat? Why not? Are you feeling well, Tori?"

She waved off his concern, not wanting to admit the real reason she hadn't eaten one of the sweet rolls was because she was trying to lose the ones she already carried in her middle. The very thought of them forced her to stand up a little straighter and suck in her gut.

"I'm fine," she lied. "Things didn't exactly turn out as I had hoped when I spoke with Mr. Sharp about the building across the street."

"Ah, yes. I've heard about him and thought that might be a problem. Perhaps I can help you, Tori. I could always purchase the building for you."

"Oh, no. I couldn't ask that of you. You've already done so much. Besides, I want to do this on my own."

"Are you sure?"

"Yes, and anyway, it's not like I'm not already living my dream. Coming out here to Noelle has been so good for me. I just didn't know how exhausting it would be."

"Perhaps you should go lie down," Nacho suggested. "You've already done so much with getting up in the wee hours for the early morning rush. Speaking of which, the breads you baked for breakfast have all sold out."

The tone of approval in her cousin's voice made Tori's heart rejoice with triumph. This morning had been the first time she baked without sampling her own work—a difficult task considering the sweet smells that beckoned she break off a morsel of the sugary crust decorating each round loaf. She had refrained, though, reminding herself that gluttony was a cardinal sin. Besides, she had eaten enough sweets to last *two* lifetimes. So, to hear that she didn't actually need to taste each thing she baked to ensure it tasted right was encouraging. Perhaps marriage wasn't completely out of question just yet.

"Thank you," she said with a bit more zest than when she first entered the restaurant. "I think I should be fine to take orders for a while, though."

"That would be wonderful," Nacho said. "The morning has been steady ever since we opened the doors this morning, and I'm sure Josefina could use some help in the kitchen."

"Oh, would you rather I help her instead?"

"No, no. I think I can manage."

The last little bit was said with a mischievous look and she could only think he was hoping he and his wife would find a few moments alone together. That's what Victoria deduced after accidentally overhearing their private conversation the week before, revealing the family they desperately wanted wasn't happening as they had hoped.

She gave Nacho a nod and swiped the pad and pen from his hand. Then she shooed him off and made her rounds to each table, ensuring each customer was satisfied with their experience before paying the bill to leave. She continued on like that for the next few hours, stopping only for brief sips of coffee to keep her energized. Finally, the last customer left and she let out a sigh of relief.

Nacho and Josefina popped out from the kitchen while she was wiping off the remaining tables.

"Whew! I feel like I danced all night long," Josefina laughed. "How was it out here, *prima*?"

"I think I dropped a whole ham," Victoria joked.

"Stop it," Josefina playfully swatted her sister-cousin. "If that's true, then you better eat two."

"Ha! Never."

Nacho only shook his head before leaning over to place a kiss on his wife's cheek. "I will never understand women. You both look fine."

A moment passed between the two newlyweds, making Victoria feel akin to an intruder. She lightly cleared her throat and they both looked up, startled.

Josefina blushed lightly. "I'll help you finish wiping down these tables."

"No, don't worry about it. I can manage fine. You two go on home."

"We couldn't do that," Josefina balked. "It's not fair to you. The dinner crowd won't begin for a few hours yet. You would be stuck here all day."

"It's fine," Victoria insisted. "I promise. I mean, I'm in a restaurant... with a built-in room to rest if I feel the need to."

"Are you sure?" Nacho asked, hesitant to leave his cousin unattended.

"I'm positive. Now go."

"Alright," Nacho said as the couple made their way to the door. He called over his shoulder, "There's plenty of leftovers in the icebox if you get hungry."

Fat chance of that happening.

Victoria only smiled. "Thank you. *Nos vemos* in a while."

"See you later," they repeated and left.

Welcoming the silence that followed, she finished wiping off the last few tables before taking the rag into the back and tossing it into a wash basin. Exhausted, she headed towards the apartment located off the side of the kitchen when the chimes on the front door clanged.

She silently groused about forgetting to lock the front door and made her way back to the dining room. "I'm sorry, but we're clos—"

Her breath catching, she skidded to a halt. Before her stood a man dressed in what had to be his Sunday finest. A light brown suit perfectly enhanced his caramel complexion. He removed his bowler, revealing thick black hair slicked back like waves. He slightly bowed.

"My apologies. I've heard good things about this place. I look forward to dining on its fare at a later date."

He placed the hat back on his head, ready to leave, when she finally found her voice.

"No, wait."

He stopped, a curious expression painting his face.

"I mean… um…" She shrugged and then laughed nervously. "Why wait?"

"Because you're closed."

"Well, yes. We are, but you're already here."

"I wouldn't want to trouble you, though."

"It's really no trouble," she maintained. "I've got food in the icebox. It will only take a moment to heat up. Please, have a seat."

She didn't even wait for him to sit, she was moving so fast for the kitchen. The door swung shut behind her and she let out a pent-up breath. She raced over to the ice box and pulled out several plates of covered foods. Hands shaking, she began removing the cloth.

What is wrong with you, she silently questioned and willed her fingers to steady as she scraped some of the food into a cast iron skillet. She stoked the coals in the stove, willing them to heat faster, and then moved on to grab a clean plate as it did so.

She hovered over the stack of dishes, debating if she shouldn't get two Talavera dishes instead. She was feeling a bit peckish and her stomach growled to remind her that it was past the noon hour and she still hadn't eaten a thing that day. Perhaps a little something wouldn't hurt. Besides, it would give her the chance to get to know this handsome stranger a little better. Maybe he would even invite her to join him.

She dished some of the food onto each colorful plate, grabbed a stack of fresh tortillas from their place in the bread box and set it all on a tray. A pair of matching mugs, also decorated in the Talavera style of monarch butterflies settling on bright flowers, were filled with *horchata*. She took a sip from one mug, briefly savoring the sweetened rice milk and then set it on the tray closest to her to avoid confusing the cups.

Placing her backside against the door, she leaned against it and pushed, all the while trying to ignore the flavorful fajitas that wreaked havoc on her empty stomach.

"Here we go," she nearly sang and turned around.

She froze.

"What did I tell you, Julieta? This town is definitely the right place for us." He awarded Victoria with a smile, who had somehow willed her feet to keep walking. She did her best to not stare at the young woman who had magically appeared from nowhere. "I didn't even have to request a second plate."

The young woman accepted her plate graciously. "Thank you, Señora."

Victoria finished serving them and stepped back, taking the opportunity to study the young lady the gentleman had invited to lunch. Of course, she would be young and beautiful. A little too young in her opinion, but wasn't that the way of some men? She fought back the ugly streak of jealousy and smiled, hoping the stranger hadn't detected the bit of disappointment she was sure to have exhibited.

"Is there anything else I can do for you?" she asked.

"Actually, yes. Perhaps you can tell us something about your lovely town," the stranger said.

"I'm afraid I wouldn't be much help there," Victoria answered. "I've only been in town about a week myself."

"How can that be?" The man pressed. "We've only been in town a few days ourselves, but already we've heard of your establishment. From what the folks say, *Nacho's Tacos* has been in business for a few years already. Although, it only really began to flourish after you came to help him."

"After I came to—" Victoria chuckled. "Oh, no. I'm sorry, sir. I fear you've mistaken me for Josefina. Nacho is my cousin... I'm not married."

A smile curled onto his face and she felt silly. Why had she added in that last part? Sigh... and especially when he was already dining with another. Still, he continued to grin like a cat that had stole all the early morning cream.

"That *is* nice to hear," he said and then quickly added, "please allow me to introduce myself. My name is Alejandro Vela and *this* is Julieta... my sister."

"A pleasure," the young woman said and held her hand out to shake.

"Sister?" Victoria mumbled, taking the girl's hand and dropping it nearly as fast when the young woman awarded her with a grin to rival the one her brother wore. "Oh, well, it's a pleasure to meet you both. My name is Victoria Villanueva. Welcome to Noelle."

"Thank you," they chorused. The girl gave her brother a knowing smile and then focused on her food, leaving the two adults to continue their discourse.

Now that it seemed the Señor Vela wasn't spoken for, Victoria felt a tad elated again. She smiled cheerfully. "I'm sure you'll enjoy it here. The townsfolk have all been kind to me. Well, at least most of them have."

"Oh? Are there any in particular that we should be wary of?"

Victoria didn't take much to the idea of being a *chismosa*. However, it wasn't really gossip if what she shared was done so in the spirit of being helpful. Right? She leaned over and lowered her voice.

"Well, I'm not really the sort to speak badly of others, but I will say that you might find things a tad difficult if you ever have need of the land office. The gentleman there has some say regarding the real estate here in town. You might not find it as easy as you hope to purchase property. I mean, if that's your sort of thing. It was mine and, needless to say, things haven't quite worked out in my favor."

"Oh, I'm sorry to hear you've had trouble with Mr. Sharp. I find it quite curious, though. He was nothing but helpful when we conducted business earlier."

"You conducted… business?"

"That's right." He took a sip from his cup and set it down again. Then he gave her a smile that warmed her from head to toe, only to be splashed cold again with his next words. "I plan on opening up a sweet shop. So, I purchased the building across the street from here—the one next to the sheriff's office."

CHAPTER 2

*O*ne minute they were politely conversing.

The next, Alejandro was wearing his cup of *horchata*.

He jumped up the moment the sweet rice milk hit him. "Woman! Are you insane?"

Victoria only stood there staring at him, her face coloring from pale to bright red. A range of emotions played on her face and he could read them all. The one that surprised him the most, though, was her anger. A bit of his own flared then. He pushed back his seat and stormed to the door, yanking it open only to turn back and give her a solid piece of his mind.

"I don't know what kind of business you people think you're running here, but it won't be around long. You can bet your sweet face on that!"

He motioned for his sister to follow and she did, grabbing a tortilla to go before scrambling after him.

Victoria marched after them. "You didn't pay for that!"

He stood in the middle of the street and yelled back at her, garnering the attention of folks passing by. "For as much as this suit cost, you'll not get a dime out of me!"

Then he turned again and raced the rest of the way across the street to the new building he had just purchased. He dug a key out of his pocket and unlocked the front door, opening it only long enough for his sister to enter before closing and locking it once again.

The teen opened her mouth to say something and he quickly raised a hand.

"Not a word, Julieta. Not one single word."

She shrugged and took off to the back of the store where he heard her take the stairs by twos, until reaching the upstairs apartment.

Alejandro sat on one of the boxes he had moved in before quitting for a lunch break. However, had he known of the kind of welcoming he was to receive at the diner across the street, he would have continued working instead. There was a lot to do before the grand opening of *Vela's Sweet Spot*, and little time to do it. He had to set up shop before the railroad came through. That was, after all, why he was here. Otherwise, he would have remained in Santa Sierra—a town not more than maybe fifty miles away. However, the railroad company had decided that Noelle was the better town to build through. As soon as folks in Santa Sierra heard of the news, they started pulling up stakes, leaving the place a near ghost town with the new moniker "Spooky Sierra." That forced Alejandro to pack up, too. He knew the railroad meant money, and that's exactly what he would need if he was going to properly care for his sister.

And his mother.

Thinking of her made him think of that woman, Victoria, again. He had heard of crazy women before, but never had he had the experience of actually dealing with one. Not even his own mother—who was being cared for back east in New York's finest sanitarium—had ever gone so far as to actually *attack* a person.

13

Alright. Maybe attack was too strong a word. It wasn't *too* far off, though.

"I hope you don't expect me to clean up that mess."

"What?" Alejandro's head snapped up. He hadn't even heard Julieta come back down—a fact that further raised his suspicions that she was sneaking off when she wasn't supposed to. Twice now he had woken on an early morning to find her missing from her bed only for her to later explain how she had gotten up early to do chores.

Except none of the chores ever seemed to get done.

He looked down to where she pointed and grimaced at the puddle soaking into the wood floors.

"No, I don't expect you to clean this."

"Good. Then I'm off."

"Off? To where?"

"It's a new town, *hermano*. I'm going to learn more about it."

"I don't think so, *sister*. You're not traipsing around town without me."

"Ugh. Come on, Alejandro. I'm not a child anymore. I'm seventeen. Plenty of women my age are married by now!"

Alejandro cringed at both the word "women" and the idea of Julieta married. Perhaps she wasn't as young as he thought, but the ten-year gap between their ages made it seem like she was still his baby sister. Perhaps he would always consider her such.

"Don't you worry none about marriage," he said.

She only crossed her arms and tapped a foot, hotly glaring at him. "Don't try changing the subject."

Young or not, she was sharper than a whole drawer of kitchen knives. Was it any surprise she had finished her schooling two years ahead of schedule? He sighed.

"Alright, alright. You can go." She squealed with excitement which he quickly waved back down. "On two conditions."

"Anything. Name them."

"First, I want you back before dark. Deal?"

"Yes, sir."

"Second, stay away from the loonies. That includes *that* one." He pointed out the shop window to the restaurant across the street. "Got it?"

"I don't think she's crazy," his sister contended.

"Are you serious? Were you even paying attention to what happened? She dumped *horchata* all over me. It's *still* all over me."

Julieta snickered. "Yeah, you should have seen your face when it happened. It was hilarious."

"You think so?" He squeezed some of the liquid off his shirt and flicked it at her. She squealed.

"Stop it!"

"Well, that's what you get for siding with a complete stranger over your brother."

"A complete stranger who had just had her heart broken," Julieta countered.

"Heartbroken? What are you talking about? I've never met the woman before in my life. I can promise you, *hermanita*, there is no attachment there… and there never will be."

"Spoken like a true gentleman," she mumbled and brushed past him.

He frowned, watching as she strode out the front door and down the street until out of sight.

Alejandro sighed. How had she grown up so much? *When* had she done so?

And what in the world was she talking about?

Broken hearts indeed. The only thing around there that was broken was his focus to succeed. It was time to get back on track, though. First, a bath to get the sticky mess off of him. Then…

He looked around the shop, taking inventory of all he had yet to do if the shop were to open on schedule. It was a Monday and he wanted to have it up and running by the following week. That way men rushing off to work and women going about their daily shopping would see a new store ready for patronage.

Despite the sticky mess all over his clothes and skin, Alejandro had to grin. His plan was perfect really. Who didn't enjoy sweets? The Puerto Rican pastries and chocolate confections his mother had taught him how to make as a child were sure to delight the townsfolk. Gone were the days of selling on the street corners of Manhattan, though. He was no longer a little brown scrap chasing down folks on the streets, begging them to buy a bon bon or two. Now they would come to him, and he would earn enough money to not only take care of Julieta but to get his mother the proper care she needed.

He nodded assuredly. It would work.

It *had* to.

He took one last look around the soon-to-be sweet shop and made his way upstairs to change his clothes. After briefly washing up, he was downstairs again and plunging whole-heartedly into the work set out before him. He unpacked one box after another, putting away the heavier items he knew his sister wouldn't be able to help move. He left some of the smaller ones—like the mixing utensils and bowls—for her to decide their appropriate places. Satisfied with the progress he made, he checked the time on the pocket watch he carried —the only thing of any real value that had been passed down from his father—and decided to step out for a brief while.

Locking the door behind him, he remembered passing a hardware store when they first arrived a few days prior and swung left, past the sheriff's office next door and Cobb's Penn & Grocery thereafter, all the while making sure to keep his eyes adverted from Nacho's Tacos. It would be too soon if he ever saw that Victoria woman again—which he was sure would happen since their businesses were across from one another. Rather, the establishment where she worked since it wasn't actually *hers*.

Much to his chagrin, he was still thinking about her when he arrived at Sheridan's Hardware Emporium. Why was her face engraved in his mind... and why in the world was he starting to buy that nonsense his sister had said about breaking hearts? Alejandro was many things, but a cad was not one of them. What had he said to upset the woman so?

He played the conversation over in his mind again.

She mentioned something about Mr. Sharp being a less than amiable individual to conduct business with. Alejandro confessed that he had encountered no problems at all when he did business with the man earlier that day.

What was the problem here? Surely, the woman couldn't be upset with him for getting along with one of the townsfolk who irritated her. No one could be *that* egotistical. What else could it be?

He was still pondering the possibilities when he reached Sheridan's.

Entering the store, he knew he was in the right place for whitewash. He pushed away any thought of the incident over lunch and approached the counter.

"Good afternoon, sir. I'm hoping you can be of assistance?"

A tall, lanky man with dark blonde hair and a matching handlebar moustache flashed a smile that lit up his light brown eyes like golden embers.

"Indeed, sir, I most certainly can. The name's Sol... Sol

17

Sheridan." He reached over the counter and Alejandro accepted the warm greeting.

"Good to meet you, Sol. Vela's the name—Alejandro Vela. I'm just in from back east and have bought a little shop in need of repairs."

"Back east you say? Sounds a bit like New York to me."

Alejandro overlooked the slight lisp hanging off the man's words, genuinely impressed he had guessed where he hailed from. The chime of the front door barely registered as he leaned against the counter, looking forward to the opportunity of making his first real acquaintance in Noelle.

"That's right," he said. "Manhattan to be exact. Not originally, of course."

"Oh, no?" Sol briefly nodded at a few browsing customers and then returned his attention to Alejandro. "Where're your people from?"

"Puerto Rico. It's a small island in the Carib. Ever hear of it?"

"I sure have. Quite a few people from there living in New York right now."

"That's right. Sounds like you might have some firsthand knowledge about that."

"Yeah, I get around some. Lived back east before realizing the west is where the real money's at. Know what I mean?"

"Indeed, I do. That's what brought me out here, too. We had just arrived in Santa Sierra when we learned the railroad decided they were building through Noelle instead."

"Yeah, bad business that—for the folks in Sierra, I mean. I've heard most everyone's pulled out of there."

"'Tis true. That's why I'm standing here before you today. You can't have a business where there's no customers."

"And what kind of business might that be?"

Sol wore an amiable grin, but Alejandro knew the sharp look in his eyes. Friend or foe, is what the man wanted to know. Was Alejandro going to build a business that competed against the man's own hardware store?

"The friendly kind," Alejandro pleasantly replied. "I'm opening up a sweet shop a few buildings down. That's why I came in today. The place could use some sprucing up. Maybe a coat or two of whitewash?"

"Well, then, you most certainly came to the right place, friend. I've got a couple of pails of that in the backroom. Give me a minute and I'll grab 'em for you."

"Thank you," Alejandro said and the man took off. He returned a couple of minutes later holding two tin pails.

"This ought to do it for you. Are you going to open an account?"

Having learned it was never good to be indebted to anyone, Alejandro declined. "I think I'll go ahead and settle up now."

"Very good," Sol replied and rang him up as the door chimed again.

Alejandro collected the two cans, nodding his thanks one last time before turning to leave...

And running straight into Victoria Villanueva.

Paint from one of the buckets splashed up, coloring the front of her calico dress with the thin white liquid.

"You did that on purpose!" she squeaked.

Her accusation forced Alejandro to snatch back the apology he had been ready to issue. "I most certainly did not! What you did this morning... *that* was done on purpose. This was an unfortunate accident."

"Much like it was only an 'unfortunate accident' that you bought the building I had bid on?"

"The building *you* bid—"

Alejandro stopped and thought back to everything that had happened earlier. Now it was all beginning to make sense. The man who drew up the deed to the place had mentioned another

19

bidder, along with some snide remark about some women not knowing their place. Considering all his mother had done to raise two children on her own, Alejandro hadn't really agreed. However, he hadn't disagreed either and turned a deaf ear to the rest of the conversation just so he could be finished with the transaction. Now this woman in front of him proclaimed *she* had been the counter buyer. No wonder she was so upset with him. Although, it still didn't excuse her earlier behavior.

The tapping of her boot against the floor brought him out of his reflections.

"I see. You think I purposely bought that building out from under you. Is that it?"

"I *know* that's what you did."

"And why, pray tell, would I do a thing like that?"

"Are you serious? It isn't exactly a secret. My cousin has told the whole town my plans. Every patron to enter *Nacho's Tacos* has asked about the *pan* I bake, wondering where they could buy batches of the bread, and we have all told them the same thing—when my bakery opened across the street."

"Well until today, I have never entered your cousin's restaurant. So, you cannot blame me for not knowing."

Victoria clucked her tongue at him. "Are you telling me you don't speak to anyone in town? Doesn't seem neighborly at all."

"How can I be neighborly? I've been in town three days, *mujer*."

"I have a name and it is not 'woman.' It's Ms. Villanueva to you, sir."

"I'm sorry, but could the two of you take your conversation outside?"

They both looked up to find Sol Sheridan nervously twisting his moustache. Victoria glared at Alejandro and then, without another word, stormed out of the store. Carefully balancing carrying the cans so that no more paint would spill, Alejandro followed after her, believing they would continue their conversation. However, Victoria was already racing back up the street.

He picked up the pace.

"So, that's it? You won't even allow me to have my say?"

She spun around.

"Perhaps you haven't noticed, but I'm dripping in paint."

"Well, then, I guess that makes us even."

"Makes us even?"

"*Sí.* You poured *horchata* all over my new suit."

She flinched and looked away, her cheeks turning a rosy red.

"That is true... and I was wrong for reacting so poorly. However, it was too much of a coincidence that you planned on opening a sweet shop in the same place that I planned on opening a bakery. Moreover, there is a big difference between spilled milk and paint."

She had a point there. The milk would wash out easily enough. Her dress would be completely ruined if she didn't rinse it out soon.

He sighed. "And I apologize for that. Although, it really was a mistake. I didn't realize you were there. Why were you standing right behind me?"

Her cheeks glowed even brighter. "I may have followed you."

His brows raised. "You followed me?"

"Yes," she admitted. "The more I thought about it, the worse I felt about my behavior. I thought I'd go over and apologize, but then I saw you leave and head down here. Really, though, I don't know why I didn't just wait until you returned to your shop."

He couldn't help but smile. She was rambling now,

looking down at her hands as if her fingernails were of some great interest. It was adorable really.

Adorable? Oh, no.

No, no, no, no, no.

He had to get out of there.

Alejandro cleared his throat. "Yes, well, apology accepted. I hope you can do the same and forgive me."

"Of course."

She beamed brightly at him and his heart did a little flip, confirming that he was swimming deeper into troubled waters.

He *really* had to get out of there.

"Wonderful. Now, if you'll excuse me, I must be going. These paints are getting a bit heavy."

"Here," she reached out. "Let me carry one."

"Nonsense. I couldn't let you do that," he said and her expression fell flat. "I meant, you already have so much to see to—with cleaning your dress and all."

"Oh," she glanced down. "Yes, I suppose you're right."

An awkward silence developed.

"Right," he said.

"Yes," she agreed.

They both began walking away only to realize they were walking side by side in the same direction.

"After you," Alejandro said and hung back.

She nodded at him and then scurried off.

It wasn't until she had completely disappeared from sight that he realized he had been glued to the same spot, watching her with awe as she swayed down the street.

He groaned softly. Why did it feel like his life was about to become even more complicated? More importantly, why was he suddenly hopeful Victoria would be the reason?

CHAPTER 3

"It's complicated," Victoria explained.

"How can it be complicated?" Nacho argued. "Did you or did you not throw horchata all over a paying customer?"

Victoria sighed. Was she ever going to live down yesterday's fiasco?

"That's not exactly right," she explained. "He wasn't a paying customer."

"Any chance that might have something to do with the fact that you attacked him?"

"I did no such thing! It wasn't an attack. I was provoked."

Nacho crossed his arms, an expression of disbelief etched deep into his face. Victoria looked over at Josefina for help, but the newest Villanueva only shrugged her shoulders, her hands raised as if to silently indicate she wanted no part of this argument. There was no way she was going to choose between her husband and new cousin.

"I have to go check on the customers." She excused herself from the kitchen and headed back out to the dining room.

Victoria wasn't about to back down, though. She had already made her apologies to Alejandro and things seemed somewhat squared between them. She mimicked Nacho's stance, arms crossed in front her chest. "What do you know of this anyway? What occurred yesterday was between Señor Vela and myself. It's nobody else's business."

"Well, it's certainly *my* business when patrons are requesting their food to go because they're afraid the staff might take their frustrations out on them."

"A patron said that? How would they even know about what happened?"

"*Prima*, you've got a lot to learn about Noelle. News travels fast around here. The whole town is talking about 'The Battling Bakers.'"

The Battling Bakers?

"That's not right," Victoria protested. "He's not even a baker. He's opening a sweet shop. I think that means candy— not cakes or the like."

Nacho sighed with frustration. "You're missing the point, Tori. This could develop into a problem for the café. If folks are afraid to come in to eat, they might decide to stop coming altogether. Already Josefina and I are struggling a bit with the town's growth."

"That should be a good thing, though. More people should mean more customers."

"Not necessarily. A lot of women are coming into town and marrying up all the men who used to make their way here for their meals. Now they're eating at home with their new wives—especially those in a family way. Sure, we still get plenty of couples coming in and others, too. However, the larger these families grow, the less likely they'll have extra funds for eating out. I'm not saying that will happen anytime soon, but I have to be mindful of the future and the possibilities it contains. Bottom line, scaring off customers is bad business."

Victoria lowered her arms and her head. "You're right, of course. I don't know what I was thinking. I guess it was simply a combination of having dealt with Mr. Sharp on top of hunger."

"Yes, that's something else I've noticed lately. Actually, it was Josefina who did and she mentioned it to me. You haven't been eating much lately. Have you been feeling ill?"

Victoria wasn't about to admit the concerns she had about her weight to a man—especially when it was her cousin. Even if he agreed, he would never say so. He would think it his duty as family to ease her worries—the same as he hovered over her like a big brother. She supposed it could always be worse, though. She actually had one of those—an older brother—and he wanted nothing to do with her, or any other living soul for that matter. Surely, the man could be found somewhere under a barrel in some bar, dousing himself with whatever rotgut available. Nacho and Josefina were really the only *true* family she had left. If her biological brother didn't want to play the role of provider and protector, who was she to complain about Nacho's overprotective ways after putting her up in this strange new town?

"I'm fine," she finally answered. "I've just lost my taste for a few things lately. I suppose everything that happened yesterday kind of took away any appetite altogether."

"I'm sorry if I came off a bit harsh about it."

"No, it isn't you. It's me. I'm just..."

She had to be blushing. She simply knew it. Her face felt like it was set ablaze when simply thinking about Alejandro Vela.

Nacho cleared his throat. "This fellow who was in yesterday—the one you threw the drink on... What did he look like? Could you describe him?"

"Oh, well, I suppose it's a bit hard to say. He looked like any other man, really. Tall, but not too tall. Perhaps only several inches taller than me. He had broad shoulders, too." She smiled then, remembering smaller details. "He had deep brown eyes—so deep, in fact, I could hardly make out the black rim outlining his pupils. Really, though, that only added to how hands—"

She stopped, her breath catching. A strange grin slid onto her cousin's face.

"Well, we will remedy this situation today, *no?* Then you will be feeling like yourself again."

She hesitated. "What do you mean? What kind of 'remedy' were you planning on?"

"You'll see... after lunch."

Nacho nodded with satisfaction, a strange smile on his face as he made his way back out to the dining room, leaving Victoria to wonder—and worry—about what her cousin had in mind.

∼

"*Mira, Alex!*"

Alejandro glanced over to where his sister pointed, a range of emotions warring inside him. His first thought was that Victoria was a vision of beauty, her green dress making the flecks of green in her brown eyes flicker like tiny emeralds caught in the midday sun. A charming curl had worked its way out of the knotted up do she wore, adding even more to her allure.

The only problem was the gentleman whose arm she clung to.

Alejandro's original desire was thoroughly doused with displeasure. He dropped the paintbrush he held into the nearly empty bucket of whitewash and picked up a rag to wipe his hands.

"*Buenas tardes,*" the man called out from halfway across the street.

"Good afternoon," Alejandro replied. Although, he wasn't so confident it was anymore.

Why did he become attracted to a woman already spoken for? In fact, why was he thinking about *any* woman at all? He knew the town's reputation of true love and mail order brides. Heck! That was why the train was coming through here instead of Santa Sierra, stealing away all its business—which was why he had come to Noelle. Right? He stared hard at the approaching couple with resolve. He had no one to blame but himself for allowing a pretty face to turn his head. "As you can see, I'm a bit busy. What can I do for you folks?"

"Ah, yes. I can see that. You're doing a very fine job there, my friend."

"Thanks." Alejandro tried to sound amiable, but couldn't muster up the feeling. He wanted to draw a definite line in the dirt and explain they weren't friends. He didn't want to spend time with anyone who would only serve as a reminder that he couldn't pursue Victoria as he had finally resolved to do. All morning long he had worked, excited about the idea that she would see his progress and maybe be just as excited. After all, she had been willing to help him the day before. What if something more came of it? What if they could be partners? Although, the kind of partners he was thinking about had less to do with the kitchen and more to do with other rooms in the upstairs apartment.

Stop! He quickly squashed his thoughts.

"Well, we understand that you're busy. Really, we only came to clear up a little matter about yesterday."

"What about yesterday?"

The man cleared his throat, arching a brow at Victoria. She rolled her eyes, huffing. However, she then looked at Alejandro and her eyes widened, all doe-like once again. There was no denying it. She was attracted to him, too. At least, that's what he wanted to think until he reminded himself once again that she was taken.

She wrung her hands. "Again, I'm terribly sorry about what happened. I suppose I can have a bit of a temper some-times—especially when I'm not thinking clearly."

"It's alright," he said softly. "I understand the disappoint-ment you must have felt. Believe me. I've been there before. So, you don't have to keep apologizing to me."

"Good," the man cut in. "In fact, it is wonderful. To show there are no hard feelings, we would like to propose some-thing of a partnership."

"A partnership?" Alejandro looked from one to the other. The man seemed highly enthusiastic about whatever was going through his mind. Victoria, on the other hand, looked embarrassed.

"I don't think he'll like the idea," she said.

"What idea is that?" Alejandro asked.

"Victoria can work for you," the man declared triumphantly.

Alejandro grimaced. Was this something he even wanted? No, he didn't think it was a good idea for him to be in such close proximity to her on a regular basis. He simply didn't trust himself. That wasn't to say he would do anything vulgar. He treated women with respect. At the same time, he was only a man. Whether or not Victoria was already in a relationship, chances were good he would eventually say or do something to make their professional one uncomfortable for both of them. It simply wouldn't do.

"Thank you for the offer, but I prefer to work alone."

Victoria's eyes widened and she quickly looked away. "There. He's decided. Let's go."

Her dejected behavior made him wonder if he had said the wrong thing. Still, he wasn't about to change his mind. He was sure working together would be disastrous for both of them.

"Wait a minute," her companion said. He turned to Alejandro. "Sir, I don't think you understand how much this will help your business. Victoria is a good, strong worker. Just look at her."

Anger coursed through his body when the man squeezed Victoria's arm and then patted her on the back as if a mule, or some other animal used to physical labor. His mood blackened even more when she blushed—her cheeks the color of the palest roses in all of the hothouses back East. Obviously, this man was like the many who had darkened his mother's stoop in Manhattan—predators in search of a free meal.

"I do fine on my own," he gritted out the words through clenched teeth. He didn't add that he thought Victoria could as well, even though he did. Instead, he raised his head in challenge. "In fact, I do the *best*."

The man's demeanor immediately changed. "Oh, *sí*... You think you are the best?"

That wasn't exactly what Alejandro had meant, but the assumption would do if it was going to get him what he wanted.

"That's right."

"Well," the man's eyes narrowed into two tiny slits. He glanced over at Victoria, who suddenly looked as if someone had stolen all her joy.

Alejandro immediately felt sick. Was this man the sort to torment his woman for failing to live up to his expectation... or was her sudden sorrow Alejandro's fault?

"I don't think your business will do as well as you think," the man suddenly declared. "Not when Victoria opens her own shop."

Victoria gasped—a reaction Alejandro almost mimicked. He wouldn't back down, though. He thrusted his hand out.

"Then may the best business win."

The man gave him a haughty smile.

"That should be easy enough. I already have all the customers. I only have to keep them."

Alejandro's mouth dropped open with surprise. "What?"

The man didn't answer, though. He only turned on his heel and stormed away—Victoria fast on his heels, throwing a cursory glance back at him before rushing onward.

Alejandro stood there, staring after them and wondering how the man already had 'all the customers' until Julieta's small—but demanding—voice sounded from behind him.

"What on earth did Señor Nacho ever do to you?

"Señor Nacho?"

"Yes, you know, the owner of Nacho's Tacos?"

Alejandro slapped his forehead, groaning.

"Wait a minute. You mean you didn't know?"

The smirk on his kid sister's face made him feel even more foolish. "How in the world was I supposed to know? I thought maybe he was a suitor or something."

An even larger smile spread across the young woman's face.

"Why are you looking at me like that? Stop it."

She laughed. "Oh, this is going to be interesting. My older brother is smitten with a woman whose family has just declared war."

"Calm down," he mumbled and picked up the paintbrush once more. He wanted to protest on all accounts. However, he knew anything he said to contradict Julieta would be a lie. The truth was that he had indeed challenged the owner of

Nacho's Tacos and the man had accepted. Worse, he was puzzled how his heart and head were in such conflict with one another...

And how Victoria Villanueva was at the root of his inner turmoil.

CHAPTER 4

$\mathcal{T}$here was a line clear out of the shop. It curved
onto the boardwalk, making its way towards the
sheriff's place next door. Victoria couldn't help but shake her
head. She didn't know what in the world Alejandro Vela was
selling at his place, but from her place at the front window of
Nacho's Tacos, she could tell the folks sure seemed to enjoy
what he was offering. In fact, there had hardly been a
customer in the restaurant all day. It didn't bother her so
much, but she could tell her cousin was terribly worried.
While Victoria had spent the past week watching the
passersby—not wanting to admit that it was really Alejandro
she enjoyed catching glimpses of—Nacho had spent that
same time falling into a deeper depression than he had the
first day they returned from their brief interlude with the
Velas. Today wasn't much better. The lack of customers had
brought about the decision that they close the diner early.

"Don't worry, *amor.*" Josefina tried soothing her worried
husband. He sat at one of the empty tables, head hanging
over an untouched cup of café con leche. By now, the sweet-

ened coffee had surely grown cold. "It's only natural that he should have so much business. After all, it's only been a week since he's opened the shop. The people will grow tired of sweets eventually, though. Then they'll return. For now, it is something new to excite them."

"She's right," Victoria chimed in. "You know how people are, cousin—especially the ones that travel out west. They're looking for excitement. How exciting can a few treats from a sweet shop offer, though? The people will return when they're ready to get back to some *real* sustenance."

"That's it!" Nacho beamed. Josefina and Victoria smiled at one another until he continued. "We'll give them something new and unexpected—something that will make whatever they're selling across the street pale in comparison."

It was like he hadn't even heard the words "real sustenance" and had chosen to focus on the idea of expanding their menu instead.

"Listen, love. We don't even know what's across the street," Josefina reasoned.

"Then we'll just have to find out," her husband countered.

"And how do you propose we do that?" she asked. "You started some silly feud with the man. You can't go in there… and I won't."

"Why not?"

"Aside from the fact I don't agree with what you're doing? I'm busy making preparations for Elvira's arrival."

"But she won't be here for months!"

"Nevertheless."

Nacho grumbled incoherent words under his breath. Guilt ate away at Victoria. Here she was supposed to be helping her cousin—repaying him for all the kindness his family had offered her during her time of need. Instead, she was causing him more grief. If it hadn't been for her, the confrontation between the two men would have never occurred to begin with.

She had to do something.

"I can pose as a customer," Victoria eagerly offered.

"I don't know," Josefina protested. "Are you sure you would want to do that after everything that's happened?"

"She right," Nacho added. "Regardless of the fact that you apologized to him, he might not take kindly to you being there either."

"I guess it's a risk I'll just have to take." She tamped down some of her enthusiasm when they both gave her curious looks. "I mean, it would be nice to find out how the sweets he makes differ from my own anyway."

She didn't add the fact that she was excited to see the inside of the shop she had once hoped to claim—or the handsome owner who had bought it out from under her. Not that she could blame him. He hadn't known she was interested in the building and it really was in a perfect location. At least, it was from what she spied in her spot at the window.

Josefina cleared her throat, and Victoria knew she must have drifted off into some daydream once again.

"Are you sure that's the only reason you're interested in going over there?" her cousin grinned wildly—which only brought a frown to her husband's face.

"Of course, that's the only reason. Tori wouldn't be interested in someone like that—not after openly declaring he's better than us. The Villanuevas are a family that stick together."

Victoria didn't dare dispute her cousin—even after Josefina rejected his claims.

"*Oye, amor*," Josefina crossed her arms. "Victoria is her own woman. She can fall in love with whoever she wants."

"Don't talk crazy, *caramia*. She isn't in love with that... that... *güey*. She only met him a week ago."

"Stranger things have happened… or have you forgotten?" Josefina challenged him. It was all the argument she was going to give, though, regarding the "guy" Nacho referenced. She stalked out of the diner with the explanation of seeing to errands, and left Victoria to face her cousin's unanswered question—the one she could see written all over his face.

"You're right," she finally said, remembering the way his family had taken her in when her own parents were killed in the Battle of Puebla. That fifth of May seemed so long ago, but the memories were still dreadfully fresh. So were the ones of spending time in the Villanueva kitchen when she left Mexico to begin her new life in Texas. Without them, who knew what would have become of her? She owed it to Nacho to remain loyal. Why should that be hard anyway? Yes, she did find herself attracted to Alejandro. However, that was nothing more than a normal reaction that oftentimes accompanied the affliction of loneliness. She squared her shoulders with resolve. "I'll go over there only to find out what goods and services he's offering, and get a leg up on my own delicious confections."

"*Eso es, prima!* That's the spirit." Nacho picked up his coffee and took a large swallow. He grimaced. "Yuck. I better go make a fresh pot in case anyone comes looking for a cup. You go on and check out the competition. I'm sure we'll be able to handle things here."

He motioned to the empty restaurant, but did so with a smile. It was good to see his spirits lift a little. She gave him a nod and gathered her skirts with determination, swiftly moving towards the door and across the street to catch the tail end of the line that had been several customers longer only minutes earlier. Things were beginning to die down some—a positive sign that maybe Josefina was right.

Customers continued to exit one by one. A tall gentleman in front of her, an Elmer Copperpot if she wasn't mistaken, blocked her view from seeing into the store. However, she could easily imagine the treats that awaited inside when the incredible scent of chocolate hit her full force. Her stomach grumbled in protest, reminding her that she had barely a morsel for breakfast again. The strict regimen she had adopted for herself did leave her feeling somewhat tired. It also left her waistline a bit slimmer, though. Finally, the customer ahead of her moved inside and she was able to edge to the front of the counter. Her eyes darted between the mounds of intricately decorated chocolate balls piled high on platters and the man who was behind the counter making them. He was facing away from her, thoroughly consumed by the work at hand. The way he molded each ball and then carefully dipped it into a pot of melted chocolate with a long ladle... and then the tiny swirls and flowers decorated on each? Well, it was obvious he had a great passion for what he was doing.

A smiling face appeared before Victoria, startling her.

"Oh, excuse me. I didn't even see you there. It's Julieta, isn't it?"

"Yes, ma'am."

"Well, good afternoon then. It's a pleasure reacquainting with you."

The girl cleared her throat and spoke a little louder. "It's a pleasure to see you again, too, Miss Villanueva."

The loud announcement of her name sent Alejandro spinning around, the ladle whipping about in the process. A ball of hot chocolate flung out, landing squarely in the middle of Victoria's chest.

"*Santa Maria!*" Alejandro abandoned his cooking utensils to grab a rag and rushed around the counter. "I'm sorry. Please, let me..."

He reached out to pick the ball of chocolate off of her,

hesitating when he realized where his hands hovered. Victoria grew warm with both embarrassment and desire.

"Perhaps I should—"

"Of course." Alejandro thrusted the cloth out to her, withdrawing with equal haste when she accepted it. "Again, I'm very sorry."

Victoria cleaned off the front of her dress, attempting to laugh at the situation. "I suppose I somewhat deserve it after the welcome you got at the restaurant."

"Not true," he insisted. "I got you back with the paint. Remember?"

"Oh, really?" she giggled. "So, you were trying to spill the paint on me after all."

Alejandro scoffed. "I hope you know better than that."

"I do," she said. "I'm only trying to lighten the mood. You seemed a bit out of sorts."

"I suppose I am," he admitted. "I was hoping to do good business, but I never thought it would be *this* good. The customers kept coming all morning long. In fact, this is the first real lull we've had all day."

"Makes sense," Victoria said. "Folks are getting on with their daily routine. I haven't been here terribly long, but I've learned that the ladies like to get most of their shopping and such finished early on so they can head home. I guess they need to prepare dinner for their husbands and such."

"Must be nice. I mean, to have someone to prepare dinner and such." She cocked her head to one side and he quickly rushed on, "Not that food would be the only reason for a man to marry, of course. Julieta and I manage just fine on our own."

"Then what are other reasons a man would marry?"

Her question caught him off-guard. "I—I don't know. To be honest, I never really gave it much thought."

His answer left her feeling deflated. "I see. Well, I really only came in to see how the shop looked from the inside. You've done a wonderful job. Now, if you'll please excuse me, I wouldn't want to keep you from your customers."

She nodded at the patrons behind him who hovered around the counter, listening in on their exchange.

Alejandro gave them a sheepish grin. "My apologies for keeping you all waiting. Please, feel free to make your purchases from what we currently have available. Julieta will be happy to ring everyone up."

He gave his sister a hopeful look. She gave him a nod followed by a wink, and then set to assisting the couple of shoppers with their selections.

He turned back to Victoria. "Now, where were we? Ah, yes. I believe you were about to make your own purchase."

"Oh, I—I don't know. I've already worked so hard."

"What do you mean?"

Victoria's confidence wavered. Of all the things to come out of her mouth, why did it have to be about that? Now she had drawn even more attention to her weight. Perhaps that wasn't such a bad thing, though. Maybe Alejandro would laud her attempt to take care of herself and look good. She straightened up. "I'm trying to maintain my physique."

"Your physique?" A confused look turned into a grin that grew until a throaty laugh finally escaped. His laugh was so hard that it actually brought tears to his eyes... and hers.

"How dare you make fun of me!"

Alejandro's mirth immediately evaporated. "What are you talking about? I wasn't making fun of you."

"Then why are you laughing?" She curled her hands into balled up fists, effectively placing one on each hip. Fighting to maintain composure and not break down in tears, her voice raised an octave higher. "What's so hilarious that you should laugh at my expense?"

He was about to answer her, but clamped his mouth shut

when Julieta loudly cleared her throat. Both Victoria and Alejandro looked her way and caught sight of the remaining customers fervently watching their small squabble.

"Would you please come with me?" She looked ready to say no until he added, "I think we could better speak in private."

Victoria relented and followed him to back behind the counter, through a door that led to a rather large kitchen. She examined her surroundings, quite impressed with the way it laid out.

"I always dreamt that if I had a kitchen it would look very much like this one." She walked over to the stove and held her hand over it. When it proved cold, she ran her hand along the nickel-plated front. "Look! It even has a place to keep bread warm."

She pointed excitedly and he chuckled, the sound of it reminding her how he had been laughing at her only moments earlier. She quickly shut down, crossing her arms in front of her chest. "There you go—laughing again."

"I tend to do that when I'm happy," he said with a mischievous look in his eyes.

"So, you're telling me you take joy out of making women miserable?"

He grew serious. "Do I make you miserable?"

Her breath caught at the tone of his voice. It almost sounded as if her chosen words actually pained him. More importantly, his demeanor frightened her. Not in the sense that he would harm her in some way, but more so that he would immediately cut off all ties with her. She wasn't sure she wanted that. At the same time, she didn't want him believing it was acceptable to make fun of her.

She frowned. "I wouldn't exactly say that. Perhaps I should have used a better word. You insulted me. Yes, that's it. Insulted is the word."

He looked surprised.

"It wasn't my intention to do any such thing," he explained with earnest sincerity. "How did I insult you?"

She timidly looked down at her hands in an effort to hide how incredibly small she felt. Her voice squeaked out her reasoning. "When you laughed at my attempt to lose weight."

Alejandro stepped close to her and her head popped back up. A solemn expression commanded his face and he gently placed his hands on her shoulders. "You do *not* need to lose weight."

The low gravel in his voice caused her to look away. However, he wouldn't allow her such an easy escape into her emotions. He cupped her chin and turned her face back to him. "Why would you even think like that? Don't you know how beautiful you are?"

A throbbing beat pounded in her throat almost as if her heart had been trapped along with her breath. Not trusting her voice, she only shook her head.

"No?" he asked, his eyes growing intense.

The hand holding her chin slowly moved up the side of her face, the tips of Alejandro's fingers gently caressing her cheek. Victoria stilled, but her mind raced. Would he kiss her? She had never been kissed before. Was there something special she should do? How terrible that at twenty and three she didn't have a single clue how to respond. Maybe if she did like she had seen others.

Victoria closed her eyes, her lips slightly parted, and leaned forward... only for her stomach to suddenly sound off with the loudest growl imaginable.

She jerked back, her eyes popping open. She sheepishly grinned. Alejandro stared at her, mouth hanging open with shock. He snapped it shut.

"When's the last time you ate, *nena*?"

Her heart and mind hung on the term of endearment for

a moment. Along with never having been kissed, one had ever called her "sweetheart" either.

"Uh, I really don't remember. I had a cup of coffee this morning," she admitted with a bit of embarrassment. "I guess I was a little busy at the diner."

Alejandro frowned with disbelief. "Excuse me for speaking frank, but I don't buy that for a second. Not a single one."

She bristled. "Are you calling me a liar?"

"What I'm doing is calling you out. I've got front windows, too. Don't you think I might glance out of them now and then?"

If he was looking out of his as much as she was looking out of hers, then chances were good that he had caught her hovering in the diner window a few times, staring across the street. She decided to be bold for once.

"What were you doing looking out the window?"

"Can't a man look out his own window? I like to see what's going on in town" he replied, indignant. She sulked a little and he sighed. "Here I am getting on you about being truthful and then I go and tell a lie."

"You're lying? You mean you weren't looking out your front window, or you don't care about town happenings?"

"No. I mean, yes, to both."

"I don't understand."

Alejandro ran a hand through his dark curls. "What I mean is that I *was* looking. I was doing it kind of with the hope of seeing you, though."

"You were? Why?"

"Uh," Alejandro glanced over his shoulder and then turned back. "Listen. I don't want Julieta thinking I abandoned her when we've still got customers coming in. We'll be closing in about an hour, though. Would you care to join us for dinner later this evening?"

She tried to hide her excitement, but was sure she did a poor job of it from the way he grinned at her. "I'd like that very much. What should I bring?"

"Only your delightful self."

Victoria warmed at his words. "Are you sure you don't wish for me to bring a dish? You and your sister have been working all day. It's the least I could do."

"I appreciate that, but not tonight. I'm going to introduce you to some of my favorite dishes."

"You're going to introduce me to them? Do you mean you're doing the cooking instead of Julieta?"

"That's right," he smiled triumphantly. "I can cook *and* make chocolate desserts."

"Sounds like I'm in for a real treat then."

"Maybe we both are," he said with a hopeful lilt in his voice.

"Maybe," she responded saucily—surprising even herself.

His eyes widened with obvious delight. "Then I look forward to this evening. Just come around to the back door. That way I'll hear you if I'm still in the kitchen."

"Very well. Until then, Señor Vela." She gave him a nod then and bid him goodbye before losing her nerve and declining the invitation. In all honesty, though, she could have sworn someone had sewn clouds into her boots as she left the shop. She floated all the way back to the diner.

"So?" Nacho asked the moment she stepped through the door. "What did you see?"

"The most amazing chocolate creations ever!" She excitedly reported back every little detail she could remember, expressing her delight several times over. "He really does have quite a keen concept going on with the way he makes the chocolates in front of the customers. It's fascinating to watch."

"You actually saw the way he was making the chocolates?"

"Briefly."

"Do you think you could create them like he did?"

Victoria scoffed. "I wouldn't even know where to begin. That's not to say I couldn't learn, of course. It's just that I couldn't make something like he did without watching more closely."

"Hmmm. Too bad you couldn't somehow go back there and do that."

Victoria hesitated. Did she want to tell her cousin that she had plans to return there later in the evening? Perhaps that wouldn't be so wise. Nacho would expect her to learn more about Alejandro's business—which wasn't too great a problem since she wanted to learn more, too. However, she didn't want to use the knowledge she gleaned simply to compete against Alejandro. After their warm exchange back at the shop, she knew there was something between them and she wanted to see it grow. Helping her cousin would make it fizzle and flop.

The bells on the diner door chimed from behind, saving her from any further conversation on the matter.

"I have returned with the mail," Josefina sang. She waved two letters in the air. "And you're not going to believe what came in it."

"What is it?" Victoria and Nacho asked in unison.

"One is from my cousin Elvira. Looks like she might be arriving sometime in September or October," Josefina beamed. She held out the second envelope to Victoria. "The other letter is for you."

Victoria looked down at the sloppy penmanship scrawled across the front. She tore open the envelope with nervous hands, her right eye twitching as she read the dreadful news.

"What is it?" Josefina asked.

"It's my brother."

"What happened?" Nacho stood, hand reached out for the letter. "Is he alright?"

"Oh, he's just fine." Victoria passed the correspondence to him. "In fact, we better start setting an extra plate at the Sunday table. The letter doesn't say when, but it looks like he'll be coming to Noelle too."

CHAPTER 5

*I*f he was going in, then it might as well be *all* in.

"The rice is good."

Alejandro held out yet another spoon of food, that one full of pigeon peas in a tomato sauce flavored with cilantro and onions. "What about these? Too much salt?"

Julieta took a bite. "The *gandules* are good, too."

He reached for a plate of plantains deep fried in oil. "Great. What do you think of—"

"Alejandro, *por fa*. I've tasted your *platanos* a hundred different times. I already know they're going to taste good. In fact, it all tastes good."

"Sorry, sorry. I just want to make sure everything turns out right."

His sister grinned. "*Ay, hermano*. You must really like this one."

"I just don't want to give a bad impression... *sister*. Mexican fare is much different than Puerto Rican dishes. I want her first meal with us to be memorable."

"Oh, it'll be memorable alright. She'll remember it was the

night she got sick from eating too much. Look at all this food you made. It's enough to feed a quarter of the town!"

"Well, maybe we can store any leftovers in the ice box and then give the rest away tomorrow."

"What a keen idea. We should donate it to Genevieve. Did you know that she plans on opening a home for women here in Noelle? It'll be the Benevolent Society of Lost Lambs."

"Is that where you've been spending all your time—with this Genevieve woman?"

"Not all of it."

"Then where have you been?"

Julieta scowled. "What's it to you?"

"Excuse me?" Alejandro crossed his arms. "I happen to be your older brother—the one who helped change your soiled nappies."

His sister rolled her eyes. "Don't remind me."

"I'm serious, Julieta. I understand that you're practically a grown woman. However, that means that others will notice that, too. I don't want anyone getting the wrong idea, thinking they can take advantage of you or something."

"Well, you can stop worrying. It's not like that. I'm spending my time with other ladies—the sort with good heads on their shoulders. In fact, one of them is the good reverend's wife, Felicity Hammond."

Alejandro nodded approvingly. "That doesn't sound too bad. After all, how much trouble can a reverend's wife get into?"

His sister only nodded and he remained unsure if he should accredit her silence to simply agreeing, or holding onto a secret. There wasn't really any time to investigate further, though. A knock at the kitchen door sent the Vela siblings into a fury of last minute clean-up and dish preparations. Alejandro removed his apron, wiped his hands on a clean towel, and rushed over to the door. He glanced behind him one last time. Julieta gave him an encouraging nod and he opened the door only to stare at the vision in front of him.

With flowers pushed into a loose bun and soft curls framing her face, there was no doubt in his mind. Victoria was the most beautiful woman he had ever seen. Now, here she was ready to dine with *him*. How did he become so fortunate?

His sister cleared her throat, startling him out of his musings. "I think I'll turn in."

"Now?" Alejandro asked. "We haven't even eaten."

"Did you forget who was the taste tester, dear brother?" She gave him an innocent smile and whispered, "Don't forget to invite her in."

Warmed with embarrassment, he turned back to Victoria. "*Mil disculpas...* a thousand apologies."

He moved aside and waved her in.

"It smells incredible in here," she said and waved at Julieta right before the young woman scurried off. "I'm sorry your sister won't be joining us."

He showed her to the table and pulled out a chair. "I'm afraid I may have made one too many dishes."

Victoria sat and took in the amazing spread of dishes lined up from one end of the table to the other. "Oh, my. You've really outdone yourself. I wouldn't know where to begin."

"Allow me, señorita." Alejandro playfully bowed and then picked up a ladle. "First we begin with our staple—the white rice. Then we cover it with the beans."

"Those are the tiniest beans I've ever seen."

"They're called pigeon peas. When we were growing up, we used to throw them at the pigeons in the park." He shrugged. "We figured they were named after them, so they must have been made for them."

Victoria's laughter was like music that caused his heart to

flutter. "That's so funny. I would love to hear more about your life from before Noelle."

"To be honest, there's not really too much to tell. I was born in Puerto Rico, but don't remember anything about it. My parents left the island when protests broke out."

"There were protests? But why? Were women trying to get the vote or something? You know, that's an issue here in Colorado."

Alejandro smiled. "Yes, I know of those. I hope the women win. My mother proved that there's nothing like a determined woman."

"How so?"

"Well, she was the one who suggested we leave the island to start anew on the mainland. You see, while my mother had been blessed with a porcelain complexion, which is what it is on the island—a bittersweet blessing—my father was not so fortunate. The protests were in regards to slavery. My mother didn't want anyone treating us differently because of how my father looked. So, she made all the arrangements to come to America—while my father reluctantly followed her lead. Unfortunately, he was restless when we got here. That's not to say he didn't do his share or anything. He kind of fell into the working class, but he was never satisfied with living in the city. Then New York joined the war and the draft started. The problem with that was having the newspapers report all sorts of ills about colored folks, along with the importance of keeping them separate and such nonsense. Meanwhile, all those folks wanted was an equal opportunity to pursue their dreams or whatever made them happy— things like the vote and right to own land and such. Well, there were a lot of sympathizers with the South who didn't like all that. So, they got it in their minds to attack all the colored folks one day. Unfortunately, my father was in the wrong place at the wrong time, and... well, you know. My mother was left raising my sister and me. I grew up quick after that so I could do my job, and take care of my family."

"I'm terribly sorry to hear about your father, Alejandro, and the trials you've surely endured since. I understand how you feel."

"I don't know if that's possible—for anyone to understand. At least, not until they've lost a parent."

"I have," Victoria admitted. "In fact, I lost both of mine in the Battle of Puebla."

"My condolences."

"Thank you." She took a bite of food, thoughtfully chewing it before swallowing. "I suppose you could say my mother was also something of a force to be reckoned with."

"Really? How so?"

"Well, my father was actually French."

"I guess that would explain your eyes."

She smiled. "Yes, I got them from him. These, too."

She smiled even wider—an almost comic smile—and then pointed to where two tiny dimples had formed in her cheeks. Alejandro was almost tempted to reach out and touch them.

"Those are some nice gifts to get."

Victoria's smile drooped. "Mmm... Well, they're the only gifts I got. I didn't even get his last name since he and my mother never officially married."

"Really? Why ever not?"

"My mother was a strange woman. She said she would never allow a man to own her. In her mind, marriage meant just that."

"And what about you? Do you feel the same as her?"

Victoria blushed. "No, not at all. To be honest, I rather like the idea."

He smiled at the idea of what that would be like—

marriage to her—until the question mirrored in her own eyes and he realized that he had gotten lost in the moment. He cleared his throat. "So, what else did you inherit from your father?"

She thought for a moment. "It's hard to say if there was any more. I can tell you what I certainly didn't get—from either of them—and that is their bravado or courage. My father, for example, went to Mexico as an explorer hoping to find the lost city of Angamuco."

"Angamuco? What's that?" Alejandro was enthralled. He couldn't help but ask questions—especially after noting the sadness in Victoria's eyes. He would do anything to keep her in high spirits, including change the topic. "Is that some kind of Aztec sight or something? You know, we've got this museum in New York—it was founded only a few years back right across the street from Central Park in Manhattan Square. In fact, it's only recently been granted its own building from what my family back east tell me. Well, that's another story. So, I naturally took Julieta there to see what we could. To be honest, it was kind of boring. In fact, they were talking about closing it all down. That is, until there was talk of archeologists doing these things called expeditions to see what kind of stuff they could find—like dinosaur bones!"

"That sounds fascinating."

"Not nearly as good as finding a whole city, though. I bet your father was proud."

"That's the thing, see, my father didn't find Angamuco. He never had the chance."

"Oh, I'm sorry to hear that. We don't have to talk about it, though. I wouldn't want you to be sad on my account of being nosy."

"Interestingly, I don't find it half as distressing as I

normally would. It's kind of strange, really. I've had other family and plenty of friends inquire about them before, and I couldn't help but shut down. However, sharing their story with you isn't sorrowful at all. In fact, I find it rather soothing."

Alejandro liked the idea of him being the one she could confide in. That she found comfort, too, was a bonus. "Go on, then. Tell me more."

"Thank you," she said with a soft smile. "The thing is that my father was already there when the battle broke out. He didn't like the idea of fighting against his own countrymen. However, he liked the notion of them trying to claim what wasn't theirs even less—especially since he was in love with my mother. That's why when my mother took arms, so did he. I guess that's why I am the way I am."

"What do you mean?"

"I'm not nearly as brave as they were."

Alejandro gently rested a hand over one of hers. "I wouldn't say that. Think of everything you've had to face since you lost them, and the fact that you are who you are today. I think that's very brave."

A slight blush crept along her cheeks. "I'm not sure I'll have room for dessert with as sweet as supper is turning out."

"You'll just have to see about making room then, because I'm certain you won't want to miss what I've got in store for you."

Victoria laughed. "You'll spoil me."

"That's my secret plan." He waggled his brows at her and she laughed. "Let's finish up and I'll bring out the next course."

The conversation continued to move swiftly over the meal they shared. She explained how she came to live in Noelle, and Alejandro shared his plans with her to build a solid business and bring his mother out west. Then he explained more about his culture, their shared responsibility to family, and his favorite dishes—like the *mofongo* Victoria savored at that precise moment.

"It's of utmost importance to correctly balance the salt and garlic flavoring, because that will pull out the flavor in the plantains and fried pork."

"Sounds like you enjoy your food as much as I do mine," she said. Then she dished out delicious recipes of her own—namely sweets—that she enjoyed making, admitting that churros were her ultimate favorite.

"In fact, I've had an idea. Have you ever thought about combining *pan con chocolate*?"

Alejandro thought about the idea for a moment, wondering what it would be like to taste a fried churro dipped in some of the hot fudge he made. "You know, I think that would be a wonderful combination. We should try it!"

"What? Right now?" Victoria laughed. "You're so funny. What about dessert?"

"Well, I do have something special to give you. I suppose you could always take it with you, though. That way we can have *two* desserts, as well as try this new recipe you suggested."

She laughed again, but then quickly sobered. "I'll have to be extra careful around you, or my waistline is going to be destroyed."

He waved away her concern. "Nonsense. There's nothing wrong with celebrating a little now and then—as long as it's all done in moderation, of course. Besides, it's like I've said before... you're absolutely perfect the way you are, *nena*."

The pet name warmed her even more than the heat in the kitchen from all the cooking Alejandro had done.

"Alright," she agreed. "Let's see what we can cook up."

He chuckled, enjoying her joke as much as the idea of

them working in the kitchen together, and started pulling out various ingredients.

"Milk, eggs, butter, cinnamon and vanilla beans," Alejandro said.

"Don't forget the flour," Victoria said with a wicked little grin. Then she grabbed a handful of it and flung it at him.

"Hey!" He jumped back, but too late.

"That's for the chocolate on my dress," she declared.

He picked up on her playful tone. "Oh, really?"

Alejandro dug his hand in the burlap bag and pulled it back out, the white powder pouring all over the counter.

"Don't even think about—"

Poof!

A ball of white hit her arm, sending a cloud of flour into the air.

She gasped. "Why, you…"

Victoria reached out to grab the bag away from Alejandro.

"I don't think so!" He pulled the bag away at the same moment she latched on.

Rip!

Flour filled the kitchen, falling on them like soft powder. Their laughter turned into coughing fits. Alejandro rushed to the door and opened it wide, swinging it back and forth in an effort to air out the place. Victoria spied a dishcloth and snatched it up, fanning the small towel up and down. Slowly, the mess they had caused dissipated and the air began to clear.

Victoria gave herself a shake, brushing her dress off before turning her attention to the white powder settling on surfaces throughout the kitchen. She shook out the dishcloth. "Well, that was a terrible idea."

Alejandro swiped at his own face and chuckled. "Yeah, but worth it."

She couldn't help but giggle at the comedic way he moved his bushy brows again... and he couldn't help but draw nearer at the tinkling sound of her laughter. He took the cloth from her hands.

"You missed a spot," he said and gently brushed her cheek.

Her eyes fluttered shut. "If you keep doing that, I might—"

"What will you do?"

She visibly swallowed. "I—I don't know. What would you do?"

"You don't get off that easy," he said and gently wrapped an arm around her. His voice dropped to a low rumble. "I would do whatever you wanted me to."

Victoria's knees buckled and she slipped forward, deeper into his embrace. He smiled broadly at her. "I think this is a perfect place to start."

Releasing her only enough to caress her chin, he tenderly tipped her head up. Then he covered her mouth with his, gently cradling her as the kiss intensified. Her breath was ragged when they finally parted. Slowly, he straightened her back up, his arms refusing to completely release her as he drank in her expression of wonder.

Clearing her throat, she pulled away and he reluctantly let his arms drop to his sides.

"I'm sorry if I behaved a little too forward."

"No, it's not that. You didn't. It's just that I'm afraid I might move a little too... well... slow." She looked up at him, her face full of embarrassment. "I've never done that before."

"You've never..."

The realization of what she was saying awakened all sorts of urges in him—the greatest of which was the desire he was the only one she would ever make such a confession to. The thought of marriage briefly crossed his mind. Was that too much, too soon? No, he decided. From the tales he had heard over the past week from his customers, a good dozen or so of the most successful marriages had been with mail order brides. In fact, it was the success of those unions that convinced the railroad to build through Noelle. Surely, he and Victoria could be as successful. Beauty aside, she had proven herself kind and funny and enjoyed food as much as him. She had pride in her family, too. That much he could tell by the way she spoke of her parents, as well as her gratitude for her extended family.

Yes, she would make a wonderful wife.

Alejandro opened his mouth to suggest as much, but then snapped it shut again. How to begin?

"Victoria, there's something I think we should discuss."

The serious tone in his voice caught her attention. "Is it something bad?"

"No, I don't think so." He chuckled. "At least, it isn't if you don't mind the possibility of this happening again."

He motioned to the kitchen and the flour that had settled in the area of their little flour fight. Her breath caught.

"You mean, you want me to work with you?"

Growing a bit nervous, he scratched the back of his head. "Well, I guess you could say that I do in a way."

"Yes!" Victoria squealed. She excitedly continued, "In fact, I can start right now by cleaning this mess. Then I can come back tomorrow and—"

"What happened here?" a small voice demanded. Alejandro and Victoria turned in unison to find Julieta descending the last stair. "I hope you know I'm not cleaning it, Alex."

His sister crossed her arms in true Vela style, trying every bit to look as grown as her mama but missing the mark by a mile. Her attempt wasn't lost on her brother, though. Alejandro snapped back to reality.

What in the world had he been thinking—nearly

proposing to Victoria? He had no business of becoming interested in *any* woman with responsibilities like his still laying in the East.

"*Disculpa*, sis. My apologies for the mess, as well as for waking you up. I promise I'll do the cleaning."

"We both will. After all, it's part of my job now," Victoria crowed.

"Your job?" Julieta questioned.

"Yes, I'm to begin working here."

The younger woman smiled broadly, shooting a fleeting glance at her brother.

"Uh... tomorrow," Alejandro stammered. "I think it's getting kind of late now. We'll discuss your duties tomorrow. For now, perhaps it's best if I walked you home."

"But we haven't even had the *postre*," Victoria quietly protested.

Alejandro nearly confessed that he had already tasted the best dessert in the house, but knew it was completely inappropriate to say such things if he wasn't willing to offer her more. Besides, Julieta was still standing there like a little fly on the wall.

"Wait here," he told Victoria. Then he disappeared into the front room. He returned a couple of minutes later, holding a medium sized gold box wrapped with brown silk ribbon. "This is for you."

She reverently accepted the parcel. "Can I open it now?"

"If you wish."

Victoria set it down on the cleanest part of the counter and gently undid the ribbon. She lifted the top off, her eyes full of wonder at the several dozen generous sizes of fudge and truffles all stacked on one another. "This is too much."

"Not at all," Alejandro insisted. "I have plenty in stock and the ingredients necessary to make more."

"Can I share it with my family?"

Her consideration of others wasn't lost on him. It was also appreciated. Perhaps this could be the beginning of mending the rift between the two families.

"Please do. It's yours to do with as you wish, but I included this many with the hope that it could serve as something of a peace offering between your cousin and me."

"What a wonderful idea. I'm sure Nacho and Josefina will both be as pleased as I am. Thank you so much for thinking of them."

"I was thinking more of you, though." Her smile warmed him throughout. "Let's go home."

She blushed at his choice of words and he realized what he said.

"I meant, I'll walk you home now."

She tucked the parcel under one arm, wrapping the other one in his when he offered it to her. Together they walked out of the back door, through the alley and across the street.

"Are you sure it's safe to go in?" Alejandro asked as they approached the darkened diner.

"It'll be fine. Nacho and I have an arrangement. I stay here in the little apartment and they stay at the house."

"That's very progressive of your cousin. I'm not sure I would feel so safe leaving you all alone."

"Well, I basically insisted. Newlyweds should have their own space."

He smiled. "I swear, you must be the most thoughtful woman I've ever met."

"Maybe you make me want to be my best me."

"You do the same to me," he admitted.

He leaned forward once more to kiss her goodnight and was a mere inch away from doing so when a glaring face in the diner window caught his attention. Startled, he jerked back. "Who's that?"

Victoria turned around—half expecting to see one of her

cousins in the window, and even more surprised than she would have been to find them still there when she recognized who it was. Her elation quickly dissipated, ending the evening on a sour note.

"That's Lucas," she said with a sigh. "My brother."

$\mathcal{V}$ictoria peered through the window, watching Alejandro sulk back to his shop. Could she blame him? When he asked to meet her brother, she rejected the idea with enough force to put anyone off. She didn't know what state she would find her brother in, though. The last thing she wanted was for a belligerent drunk to run off the man she was falling for.

The thought made her smile. She *was* falling for Alejandro... and she didn't mind admitting it. Of course, that didn't mean she wanted to try to do so right now. She turned, fists planted firmly on her hips.

"What are you doing here, Lucas?"

"What am I doing here?" Her brother drawled the words out, confirming her suspicions. "What do you think I'm doing here? Didn't you get my letter?"

"Only this morning!"

"Good. Then you knew I was coming."

Victoria heaved with exasperation. "Luc, one afternoon is hardly enough time to prepare for someone's arrival."

"Especially when you're busy entertaining others," her brother countered. "Who was that anyway?"

"That was the man who owns the sweet shop across the street."

"Oh, yes. Nacho told me about him."

"Nacho? You've spoken with him?"

"Of course, I did. He and his wife, our new cousin Josefina. What do you think of her?" He waved away his own question. "Never mind that. Who do you think let me in and put up my little bag? I can't walk through walls, you know."

Only windows.

Victoria suddenly remembered a time when her brother was so determined to get a drink that he broke into a saloon by throwing a rock through the window. The smell coming off him made her sure that he would do the same in his given condition if given the chance—which she most certainly wasn't about to let happen. The last thing she wanted was for him to scare off the first man to ever show any real interest in her. Why couldn't Nacho have invited her brother back to his home? She wasn't able to stay in the new barn they had recently built, but it would have been more than suitable for her brother. She mentioned as much.

"I suppose we'll figure out a sleeping arrangement of sorts."

"Not necessary, sister dear. I can find my own lodging."

Oh, she could just see it now—her newly arrived brother, stumbling through town. Not a chance!

"What kind of hostess—or sister, for that matter—would I be if I didn't show you better hospitality than that? Besides, I'm sure you've traveled long and far. Not that I would know for certain, of course. I can't quite recall the last place you were."

"Oh, um… Out near a little place called Sweetwater. You ever hear of it?"

"Can't say that I have. What were you doing out that way?"

"Just a little of this, a little of that." Lucas hiccupped and his breathing slowed as his exhaustion grew obvious. "Real pretty place."

"Then why did you leave?"

His eyes widened, but her question remained unanswered. With an exaggerated yawn, he stretched his arms wide. "It's getting kind of late. Didn't you say you had a bed or something?"

"This way."

She showed Lucas through the kitchen, to the small apartment where she stayed. She pulled out her key and unlocked the door, opening it wide for him.

"Not too bad," he said and strode straight towards the bed. He fell back onto it, with arms crossed under his head for support and his booted feet barely hanging off the edge of the mattress. "Not too bad at all."

Victoria stifled a sigh of frustration. "Perhaps you'll be more comfortable without your boots on."

"Don't know about that. What if I was going to die? A man should die with his boots on."

"What kind of talk is that? Are you in some sort of trouble, Lucas?"

"No," he said solemnly. He kicked the boots off, one after the other. "There. You happy now?"

She knew he was lying about not being in trouble. In fact, that could have been his proper name had his parents the ability to foretell the future. Still, she didn't want to get into any arguments with him—not on such a lovely evening. Why hadn't her brother done something meaningful with his life? Six years her senior, he had been fortunate to know their father better than she. At least, well enough to have learned his native tongue. While Victoria could speak Spanish, Lucas knew both Spanish and French. Why didn't he use his skills for something useful? It just went to show how a formal education didn't necessarily make the man. In fact, Alejandro has hardly any education at all—only what he had learned in the street. Their dinner conversation popped into her mind. "Hustling" is what he had called it.

Her thoughts stayed with him and the moments they shared in his shop. Oh, how she wished she could go back to them. She would remain there forever! Really, Alejandro was properly suited for the work he did... as sweet as the box of chocolates that sat in the dining room on one of the tables.

An idea dawned on her. Wouldn't it be nice if she could make up one of the confections she had suggested earlier? Indeed, it would be a lovely treat she could bring to him the next day as her way of thanking him for a wonderful night. Speaking of which...

She glanced up at the only window the apartment boasted. Dusk descended on the town. She would have to work fast if she was going to make her creation and still find appropriate sleeping arrangements—an obvious necessity emphasized by her brother's light snore. Victoria glanced down at her brother. He had fallen asleep faster than a blown-out candle flame. All the better for her, she supposed. It would be one less thing to worry about for the moment.

Quietly, she walked over to the wardrobe and gathered a few garments. Too bad the town building being renovated into a women's home wasn't up and running yet. She guessed she would just have to see if Seamus would have room at the saloon for her. Surely, he could find a small spot for one evening... but she better hurry before it filled up with too many patrons looking for the same after they drank more than their fair share. The sooner she got to the saloon, the better she would be able to assess the situation (and get settled in, if all went well).

Victoria finished packing up her toiletries. Then she closed the apartment door behind her and made her way through the kitchen. The treasured recipe book she carried everywhere with her sat on the counter. She set her carpetbag down beside her and quickly thumbed through it, finding her favorite recipe. It was what she preferred, but she knew there wasn't any time to actually bake the dessert. But what if she could vary it a bit?

"That's it!" Victoria excitedly spoke to herself and sped out into the dining room to collect the box of chocolates and bring them back to the kitchen. She didn't have time to bake breads, but she could definitely spend a spell melting chocolate. She pulled out a match from the box they kept in a cupboard and struck it. Then she lit the leftover coals in the stove. Thankfully, they were still warm from the cooking done earlier in the day. It wouldn't take long to complete her task, and her mind immediately drifted back to the stove in Alejandro's kitchen. She wondered what it would be like to cook on it; use the oven to bake her own desserts. It would probably work even better (and faster) than the one in Nacho's Tacos. The prospect of working with Alejandro was too exciting. She couldn't wait for tomorrow!

As the stove heated up, she inspected the box of chocolates once again. There were so many pretty pieces—she was tempted to gobble one up right then and there!

"Patience is a virtue," she half sang as her fingers hovered over the chocolates. She finally settled on two pieces. One was a larger chunk of fudge and the other a delicately decorated truffle. "Yes, these will do quite nicely."

The larger piece of fudge went into a pot and then on the stove. While it slowly melted, Victoria dug through the bread box for day-old *pan* and pulled out a *corazon*, the cookie being aptly named for its heart shape design. Setting it on a piece of parchment paper, she grabbed hold of a rag and brought the pot to the table. Then she carefully drizzled the melted chocolate in a zigzag design over the flaky cookie. Setting the pot aside, she placed the pretty truffle in the center of the heart. While she waited for the heated chocolate to set, she swiftly jotted down what she had done along with plans for other sweet breads she thought would do well with chocolate drizzled over them. Then she pushed the book to the side and proudly admired her creation.

She couldn't wait to give it to Alejandro!

That wouldn't be until tomorrow, though. What if someone had the mind to eat it before then? Victoria could see it now—her brother waking from his drunken stupor, prowling through the kitchen on a search for something to eat. It wouldn't end well for her little heart... both figuratively *and* literally speaking.

She best leave a note.

Victoria searched around for the old scratchpads her cousins kept in the diner for taking down orders, and an old lead pencil.

Para Alejan—

No, she couldn't write that. There would be too many questions if she left a note indicating the pastry was for Alejandro, and she wasn't sure she wanted to answer any of them yet. Already she was going to have to find a way to sneak out of the restaurant to go to the sweetshop. Customers wouldn't be so much a worry with the way business had died down over the past week. However, there was now an extra set of eyes to spy her whereabouts.

She bit her lip, thinking about what to pen and then

finally settled for the most simple and direct thing she could think up.

Do not eat.

VICTORIA LEFT the note beside the chocolate covered cookie and picked up her bag again. Then she quietly headed out the door, locking it behind her. Turning right, she made her way down the street and couldn't help but glance across the way. With the exception of one small light in an upstairs window, the shop looked dark. It reminded her of how quickly evening was descending. The sun had dipped down below the mountains, leaving little more than an orange haze on the horizon, and the moon already loomed overhead like an inpatient child begging it's turn for attention.

She picked up the pace, thankful the Golden Nugget saloon was only three buildings down. In less than five minutes, she arrived. Pushing through the batwing doors, she ignored the stares of men who paused long enough from their imbibing to ogle her. She made her way to the bartender.

"How can I be helping you, Miss?" Seamus asked.

"Are all your rooms spoken for?"

The bartender looked a bit uncomfortable. "I suppose not."

"Then I would like to rent one for the evening."

A voice from behind her cackled. "Save your money, sweetheart. You can share mine."

Victoria furiously blushed.

"We'll be having none of that in here, Elmer Copperpot."

Seamus waved a finger at the miner. "Now apologize to the lady, or you'll be finding your drinks elsewhere."

Elmer grumbled an apology and then drowned the rest of his drink amidst laughter from the other men. Victoria didn't know if she should be angry at the man... or feel sorry for him.

"Don't you worry none about him," Seamus said. "He's all talk. In fact, he doesn't even rent my rooms. He's got his own place out a ways past your cousin's. Speaking of which, don't you stay with them?"

"Yes, I normally do."

"Well, there be nothing wrong. Right?"

"No, no. It's nothing like that. We had unexpected company arrive only a while ago. It wouldn't have been right to make them find their own housing. So, I gave up my room."

"And there be no room for you at the Villanueva homestead?"

"Well, it's getting awfully late now. Too late to travel alone all that way. Besides, I wouldn't want to wake them if they've already turned in for the night."

"Yes, I suppose that's possible. Nacho does keep somewhat strange hours at the diner for that *siesta* thing they do. Although, I have to admit I kind of like the idea of taking a break for a few hours in the afternoon." Seamus fished around in his pocket. "Alright. You say it's only for the one night?"

Victoria eagerly nodded. "That's right."

"I suppose I might have a place for you as long as you don't mind it being a bit small."

"That'll be fine." She followed him up a set of stairs to one of the rooms and he unlocked it for her inspection. She nodded her satisfaction and handed over the key. "Thank you, sir."

"Not at all. Please don't hesitate to notify me should you need anything."

She thanked him again and then retired to her room to prepare for bed. With the door soundly locked, it wasn't long before she was snuggled under the covers and succumbed to delicious dreams dancing in her head.

CHAPTER 7

*T*he best part of waking up was coffee in his cup.

Alejandro inhaled deeply, the fresh scent of ground coffee beans filling his senses. He scooped several spoons full of grinds into the boiling water, stirred and then removed the pot from the stove. Lining another pot with a cheesecloth, he allowed the liquid to drain into it as he added sugar to his cup. When the coffee was ready, he removed the cheesecloth and poured a little of it over the sugar. He stirred the new mixture until it was a thick, beige paste. Then he topped the cup off with more coffee, watching the creamy *espuma* rise to the top. He took the first sip and sighed.

"*Perfecto.*"

"Is that café I smell?" Julieta came bouncing down the stairs, into the kitchen. She made her way to where he stood and made a show of inhaling. "Aaahhh. That smells divine."

He chuckled. "Allow me."

Alejandro carefully prepared a second cup and handed it to her.

"Well, you're in a good mood. I wonder what might be the reason for that. Hmmm?"

"Hey, don't you start." He picked up a nearby cloth that still held some of the flour from the mess he had stayed up cleaning. He tossed it at her and she squealed.

"Don't you dare!"

"Then get to work," Alejandro playfully demanded.

Julieta took her cup of coffee and headed for the front room. "How many boxes do you think we'll sell today?"

"I don't know, but I bet it'll be a lot. The folks here in Noelle seem to have a real sweet tooth. At this rate, we'll move mama out here in no time."

"I can't wait!" Julieta beamed. "I feel like it's been forever since we've last seen her."

"I know it's been difficult for you, Julieta. It's been hard for me, too. However, it really hasn't been all that long since we came out west. All of our diligence is about to pay off, though. So, keep your head up. We'll see her again soon."

"You're right." Julieta nodded and then took a big gulp of her coffee. She set it down behind the counter and walked around. "Now if you'll excuse me, I think I'll go for a nice morning stroll."

Alejandro waved her away as she went to the front door and unlocked it. He went to work pulling out the ingredients and tools he would need to make a fresh batch of chocolate as Julieta opened the shop door and stopped.

"Hey, something's going on across the street."

"What do you mean something's going on across the street?"

"It looks like people are returning to Nacho's Tacos."

Alejandro shrugged. "That would make sense. They open for breakfast and we don't. People will prefer to come on over here when we open our doors in a bit."

"Are you going to have me stand outside and give away food, too?"

That caught him by surprise. He stopped what he was

doing and walked around the counter. Sure enough, the man he had spied the night before was standing outside with a tray.

"Looks like he's offering some sort of samples or something."

"Maybe I should go check it out," Julieta offered.

"What?" Alejandro asked absentmindedly. He looked back to her. "No, don't worry about it. I'll go check it out myself after I finish setting up for us to open today."

"Are you sure that's a good idea? You and Señor Nacho aren't exactly on speaking terms."

Alejandro thought about the box of chocolates he had gifted Victoria, in part as a peace offering to her family. "I think things might have changed since last night. Besides, that's not Señor Villanueva. That's Victoria's brother."

"She has a brother? What's his name?"

"Um," Alejandro thought for a moment. "I think she said it was Lucas. I don't remember entirely. It was late, so I didn't get the chance to meet him."

"That kind of gives you an excuse to go over there. Doesn't it?"

"Hey, you're right." Alejandro grinned. "I can just say that I'm going over to introduce myself since we didn't have the opportunity to properly introduce ourselves."

"Oh! I have an idea." Julieta made a dash from the room, calling over her shoulder. "I'll be back in a minute."

She disappeared through the kitchen. A minute later, true to her word, she had returned. This time, she carried a carefully folded dark brown cloth in her arms.

"What's that?"

"Open it and see."

He took the material from her and carefully unfolded it.

"Julieta, this is beautiful. When did you make it?"

She smiled with pride. "Last night. When I left you and

Victoria alone for dinner, I thought I would make something for her. An apron seemed appropriate. Now that she's going to come work for us, it seems even more so."

He gently placed the apron on the counter and fingered the embroidered name "Victoria" that sprawled across the front. On either side of the name were tiny flowers sewed into the fabric. "This must have taken you forever."

She shrugged. "Not really. I used that new sewing table you bought me."

He remembered seeing the machine in a shop back east in Manhattan. The owner selling it said that it was revolutionizing the way women made clothes, cutting the time they spent to less than half the usual amount. Alejandro figured his sister might appreciate something like that. Thankfully, she did.

He carefully folded the apron once again. "This is not only beautiful, but thoughtful. Thank you, Julieta."

He held the apron back out to her, but she only shook her head. "I want you to give it to her when you go over there."

"Are you sure you wouldn't want to give it to her yourself?"

"I think it would be nicer if it came from you." Her eyes flashed with mischief and he immediately knew what she was doing.

Little Miss Matchmaker.

"Alright. Then I think I'll go do that."

"Well, you better hurry up. Looks like that brother of hers is finished handing out whatever he had. He's going back inside."

Alejandro inwardly groused. "I don't have time to go chasing him down right now. I've still got all this to take care of." He motioned to the sweets that still needed to be set out, as well as the ones he would have to make.

"Don't worry about this. I can take over here for a bit and you can go next door."

"What about your morning stroll?"

His sister rolled her eyes. "Really, Alejandro? Sounds like someone's turning yellow to me."

He squinted at her. "*Oye, hermana.* I'm not scared of anything."

"No?" She challenged him. "Then prove it. Go over there and introduce yourself to Victoria's brother. Find out whatever it is he's offering... and bring me back a bit!"

Alejandro chuckled. "So, that's what this is really about."

She didn't respond, instead setting herself to work. Alejandro tucked the apron under one arm and walked out the front door, heading straightaway for the diner just as Victoria's brother disappeared back inside.

Alejandro reached the front door and hesitated, his hand hovering over the knob.

"Here goes," he muttered.

He walked in and noted that about half the tables were filled. No one seemed to notice him, though. Then he heard a singsong voice.

"Hello. Can I help you?"

He recognized the woman from the view in his shop's window, and could recall seeing Señor Villanueva helping her in and out of his carriage.

"You must be la Señora de Nacho Villanueva."

"Indeed, I am," the woman said with a slight accent. "My name is Josefina. Who might you be, señor?"

There was fire in the eyes, but her smile was pleasant enough. He took it as a good sign. "The name is Alejandro Vela. I own the shop across the street—the one that sells sweets."

"I see. And what is it we can do for you, sir? Did you come to dine?"

"Um, actually, I came to speak to Victoria."

"I'm afraid that's not possible right now."

He grew suspicious. "Why not?"

Josefina shrugged. "She's not here."

"Where is she?"

"I don't know. She wasn't here when we arrived."

"What about her brother?"

"You know Lucas?"

"Not really. Victoria only briefly mentioned him last night."

"Last night?" A strange look passed over Josefina's face. "*Mi prima* was with you last night?"

"No! I mean, yes, but..." Alejandro scrambled for the right words. "Your cousin only came over for dinner. My sister was there with us as well. At least, in a matter of speaking... It's not what you think."

"I can assure you I think nothing at all on the matter." The smirk Josefina wore betrayed the words she spoke. "She should be back shortly, though. Perhaps you wish to wait for her?"

"Actually, I—"

"*Tesoros!* Get your little treasures."

The kitchen door swung open and the most incredible smell of baked breads and chocolate followed Lucas out, who waltzed into the dining room with a tray balanced on one hand. A few diners motioned for him to attend their tables. A couple even stood and met him halfway.

"These are delicious," one woman declared. "I love the way the bread is so filling."

"Yes," another chimed in. "The chocolate drizzle gives it that extra something special, though."

"Especially with that cinnamon grated over it."

Alejandro scowled. He looked over to Josefina. "Since when did your diner serve chocolate?"

"Well, we've always had chocolate here. It was mostly for drinks, though. You know, *chocolate caliente*. The clientele absolutely loves hot chocolate. It never dawned on us to serve up baked goods with chocolate, though. At least, not until Victoria left us a box of chocolates and book of new recipes to try out this morning."

"Box of chocolates?"

Alejandro could feel his temperature rising. Now he understood why she had been so quick to get rid of him the night before—refusing to introduce him to her brother. It had nothing to do with the late hour, or the possible inconvenience. He had served his purpose and she wanted rid of him. How foolish he had been to gift her a whole box of expensive sweets!

His jaw grinded away, the muscles working double time as he fought to maintain his composure. He would not lose it in front of all these clients. There was still a chance to win them back—and he most certainly would. Even if it was the last thing he did, he would get even with the Villanuevas. He thought to say as much, but the bells on the front door chimed.

"I'm so sorry I'm late. I was down at the—" Victoria froze. "Alejandro! What a pleasant surprise."

Was it his imagination, or did she suddenly look uncomfortable? Yes, he supposed she would feel much discomfort now that her little secret was out. He marched up to her, willfully ignoring how beautiful she looked with her face flushed and the usual rebellious curly wisps outlining the curves of her soft cheeks.

"Well played, *nena*." His voice was low enough for only her to hear. "Well played indeed. You have fooled me once. It will not happen again."

Her eyes widened. "Fooled you? I don't know what you mean."

"Oh, no. I won't fall for your charms again. If you think that will continue to work so you can weasel more of my free *dulces* from me, then you are gravely mistaken. In fact, the only thing you'll ever get from me now is this." Alejandro held out the apron Julieta had insisted he deliver.

Victoria accepted the fabric, apparent shock written all over her face. "What is it?"

"My sister thought it would have been a nice gift for when you came to work at the shop," Alejandro explained. "Of course, you'll not be coming to work with us now that you've gotten what you want. Good luck with your endeavors."

"My endeavors? Really, Alejandro I don't understand a single thing you've said. I've never tried to weasel free sweets or anything else from you. Why are you so upset?"

Alejandro only then realized how quiet it had become in the restaurant. The diners were all staring at him. He turned away from their curious faces and stormed past Victoria, refusing to allow her innocent looks—or the call of his name —to reel him in once again. He sped across the street, fighting his desire to venture a glance her way, and slammed the door once inside the sanctuary of his shop.

Julieta looked up from her place at the counter. "Uh, oh. What's wrong now?"

"What's wrong? I'll tell you what's wrong." Alejandro quickly relayed all that had occurred.

"There must be some sort of mistake," Julieta frowned. "I can't imagine Victoria being so underhanded. Surely, this is a misunderstanding."

"Oh, there was nothing to misunderstand at all. Her cousin, la Señora Villanueva, specifically said that the recipes were Victoria's and from the box of chocolates I gifted her last night."

Julieta gasped.

"Uh, huh." Alejandro nodded. "Now you understand."

"But why?"

He shrugged. "The chocolate they use for their beverages is probably inferior to ours. Last night was the only way they could get their hands on enough of it to try out her recipes—see if it would taste good before spending money to import something similar to what we have."

"All chocolate comes from the same beans, though. The only thing that makes yours special are the ingredients you use—the cream and sugar—and the *way* in which you make it."

"Ah, yes. You and I know the real secret is found in our recipes. However, they don't know that."

Julieta sighed. "Well, no matter. They'll run out soon and we don't have to sell anymore to them. Since they'll not find anything similar to what we make—at least, not easily—we won't have to worry about it soon. They won't be able to make more and the customers will return to us."

"Yes… until they think up another ploy to steal away customers. Don't you see, Julieta? That's what this is all about. It doesn't matter if they won't be able to offer their customers more. It was about trying to take *our* customers—make things difficult for us so that we would lose patrons."

Julieta pouted. "What a lot of nasty business."

"Not to worry, *hermanita*. I've got a plan."

"You do? What kind of plan is it?"

Alejandro smiled with satisfaction. "The festive kind."

CHAPTER 8

*T*hree days. That's how long it had been since Victoria suffered both Alejandro's wrath and her brother's incompetence. She sobbed quietly. Why did he have to wake up that morning in a stupid, drunken stupor and assume the box of chocolates he found on the counter were for baking? Why did their cousins listen to him and use her recipes?

Why had her parents died in some senseless battle? Why had God equally abandoned both her and her brother—allowing him to become a pitiful drunk... and her to fall for a man she would obviously never have?

She cried once more.

So many questions and too many doubts. It was exhausting!

Lucas knocked on the door to the small kitchen quarters once more. "How can you still be upset, Tori? Now what's wrong?"

"Everything!" Victoria, sprawled out on the bed, buried her head in the pillow. Her muffled voice barely sounded out from it. She lifted her head and clearly yelled, "Go away, Luc."

Lucas turned to his cousin. "What kind of person only has one key to his home?"

Nacho shrugged. "What kind of person would need more than one?"

His cousin grunted and raised a fist to pound on the door again, his hand halting in midair when Josefina approached. "Step aside, boys. I think this will require a woman's touch."

"But why should it?" Lucas demanded. "We didn't do anything wrong. In fact, we were only trying to help."

"Well, Victoria obviously feels differently."

"*Ay, por fa…* This is ridiculous!"

His sudden outburst forced Josefina to cock her head in a way that welcomed any challenge to her decision. Nacho placed a hand on his cousin's shoulder, gently pulling Lucas away. "Uh… I think we should maybe do as she says."

Lucas gave him an incredulous look. "You can't be serious. This is *my* sister we're talking about."

Nacho chose not to point out how Victoria's welfare had been of little concern to Lucas until now. "I need help out front anyway. After all, we must keep the customers happy. No?"

"Most of them have already cleared out."

"Yes, but you never know who might waltz in at the last minute. Besides, even one alone has the power to bring in more customers or drive them away. Our service will determine what they tell their friends."

Lucas allowed himself to be pulled away at that point.

Josefina leaned in close to the door. "The boys are finally gone. You can open up and let me in now."

The seconds stretched out into minutes, leaving Josefina to wonder if she would have to find someone to remove the door from its hinges. She was about to threaten as much when it suddenly cracked open. Victoria peered through, her eyes red and puffy.

"*Ay, prima.* Have you been crying?" Josefina pushed against the door until Victoria finally stood aside and allowed her in. "You look like someone has told you it's the end of the world—especially with all the weight you've been losing over these past few weeks."

Victoria's eyes widened with false naïveté.

"Don't give me that look," Josefina continued. "Perhaps no one else has noticed, but I most certainly have. Now, come. Tell me what is wrong. Surely, it is not so bad as to waste good tears. You know what they say—you only get so many and then they're gone. Wouldn't you rather save them for something happy… like when you're an old woman and your children come to visit with their babies?"

Victoria glared at Josefina, her eyes turning into small slits. "Is that what you're doing, *prima*? Saving them for your… *babies*."

Josefina's expression fell and shame immediately washed over Victoria. "I'm so sorry. I never should have said that. It was cruel and hateful. Please forgive me."

Her cousin waved away the apology. "There is nothing to forgive. You are right in a way. I *am* saving my tears for them. You see, I still have hope that my dreams will come true— that I will become a mother one day. However, it's as the saying goes—*en el tiempo de Dios.*"

Victoria sighed. "I don't want to wait for God's timing, though. Sometimes, I think He's forgotten about me."

"Nonsense, *prima*. Don't ever think that. We don't know what the good Lord's plans are, but they are designed to help us. We simply must have faith that glad tidings await us all."

Victoria smiled. "This is the first time I've heard you

speak like this, Josefina. I didn't realize you were so religious."

Her cousin laughed. "Neither did I."

"I suppose we have our moments," Victoria said.

"We do. Perhaps this one is yours."

She considered her cousin's suggestion. Could this be her moment for happiness? She knew she wasn't particularly bold. At least, not like her cousin or the other ladies that had ventured out as mail order brides—overcoming all kinds of obstacles from cathouse madams to old hand villains, and everything between to get what they want. Maybe that was the *real* dilemma here. What exactly was it that Victoria wanted anyway?

There was little time to explore the question, though. A cry sounded from outside.

"Was that a…?"

The women looked at one another, their mirrored expressions ranging from confusion to curiosity. They both raced towards the door, opening it only to tumble into the kitchen onto a scene neither of them would have ever expected. A teary-eyed woman with sapphire blue eyes and hair the color of straw pinned into a loose bun stood before them, a baby cradled in her arms.

"He *is* your son," she cried in a Southern drawl. "Anyone who has ever seen him would tell you as much. You'd admit it, too, if you'd just stop being so stubborn. The baby is yours. Just look at him!"

Lucas refused to do as she bade. "How many men have you told the same thing, I'm sure hoping one will buy your story?"

Victoria gasped. "Lucas Villanueva! How could you say something so cruel? You were raised better than that."

Josefina slid past them all. "Uh, I think I'll just go see if Nacho needs any help in the dining room. Excuse me."

"I was hardly raised at all," her brother mumbled. Part of her understood the underlying hurt in his comment, but she wasn't about to let him off the hook that easily.

"It makes no matter. You know better than to speak to a lady like that—especially a new mother." Victoria approached the woman, her hand outstretched. "Please excuse my brother. I promise I'm not nearly as surly as he is. The name is Victoria."

The woman shifted the baby in her arms and cautiously shook Victoria's hand. "Greta. Greta Goldst... uh, Gold."

Victoria looked over at her brother who wore a satisfied grin.

"See what I mean? You can't believe a word she says."

Greta's eyes welled up. "That's not true!"

Before her brother could say anything to further upset the young woman, Victoria stepped between them. She peered down at the baby. "May I?"

Greta nodded and held the baby out to her. Victoria smiled broadly.

"I do believe you're right. The child may have your golden hair, but his face is every bit a Villanueva." She turned to her brother then and angled the baby in a way to make it easy to see his features. "Don't you think so, Luc?"

Her brother crossed his arms, his face hardening as he quickly looked away. "No."

"Well, of course you won't be able to tell if you don't look at him," she snapped. "Now act like you really are the eldest sibling and stop running away."

Sure enough, her plan of calling him out worked as she had hoped. His eyes flared the same as the day their mother's had when their town of Puebla fell under French invasion. Determination shone in them as he stepped forward, his eyes trained on her until he was close enough to see the child. Then his eyes carefully turned downward and his mouth dropped open as he stared. Instinctively, he reached out and brushed a trembling finger down the baby's smooth cheek.

"He looks like you did as a baby," Lucas mumbled.

"Nonsense," she said. "I look like father."

"You have his coloring, yes, but there is still plenty of mother in you—especially when it comes to that temper of yours."

"I don't have a temper," Victoria protested. Her brother looked at her with skepticism and she sheepishly grinned. "Well, only on occasion."

"No one is perfect." He glanced over to Greta then. "Including me."

Greta's face filled with hope. "I'm not asking for perfect. I'm just asking you try to be there. Can you do that?"

Lucas peeked down at the child once more. "I can't make any promises, but I'll do what I can."

The woman beamed brightly at him.

"Can I have my kitchen back?" Nacho stood in the doorway. He entered the kitchen and it swung shut behind him. "I know I don't have a lot of clients at the moment, but I do have some and need to get in here so I can cook for them."

"Our apologies, *primo*." Victoria tried handing the child to her brother, but he backed away. Fearful of pushing Lucas too hard, too soon, she passed the baby back to his mother. She returned her attention to Nacho, who quietly studied them all. "I guess you never thought I would come with so much... baggage... when you agreed to take me in."

"Nonsense," he said. "We are all family here. Family sticks together through the thick of it all—kind of like you did for us when you brought back that box of chocolates."

Victoria sighed. "Nacho, that wasn't meant for you. At least, not like that. It was a peace offering that Alejandro had gifted me—his way of apologizing for his part in the small feud between the two of you, as well as a way of inviting me into the fold."

"Inviting you into the fold? You mean... Victoria, have you two reached an understanding?"

For that her brother did turn around. "You're getting married?"

"What? No!" She didn't add that she wished it was an option. That possibility was long gone now. Lucas's eyes grew wary as Nacho careful watched her. She cleared her throat to offer a better explanation. "It wasn't *that* kind of understanding. I was going to work for him."

Her cousin's mouth fell open. "What? Why would you do such a thing? You have a perfectly good job here, baking the breakfast *pan*."

Victoria glanced over at her brother, but saw she would find no help over there. He was lost in his own world, he and Greta holding a quiet conversation of which she could only catch a few mumbled words.

"For as much as I enjoy baking bread here at the diner, I have dreams of my own, Nacho. That doesn't mean that I care any less for my family either. I wanted to say that since I know family means a great deal to you. It does for me as well. However, I don't want to feel like I'll be forever indebted to mine simply because they stepped in during a difficult time in my life. I was a child saddled with an unfortunate circumstance. I don't want to follow that pattern as an adult."

"I would never think you owed me anything simply because you stay here."

"Are you saying that you never once thought of me working here at the diner as equal to me earning my keep... or that you didn't wish for me to get closer to the Velas just so we could know what they were offering the townsfolk?"

Nacho rubbed the back of his head, a hangdog expression

on his face. "Alright. Perhaps I did think those things a little bit. I didn't mean any harm by it, though. I only got caught up in the moment of it all, trying to save my restaurant from going under. Now you say you're going to help facilitate that by quitting and going to work for the competition, but not for any reason other than the fact that you want to strike out on your own. Family should stick together, though."

"I'm sorry you see it that way, but I disagree. You all are my family and will always be important to me. However, the Velas are not competition. If anything, they could be allies."

"Allies? How so?"

"Simple. He isn't open during the early morning hours like the diner is. Perhaps you could buy chocolate from him to bake into your breakfast breads, using a few of the recipes that I've created." She took a breath, decidedly omitting that the other recipes would be for Alejandro. They weren't ones her cousin could use anyway. "When the customers express their delight, you can explain where the chocolate comes from and, since you don't offer much of a dessert menu here, you can direct them to the shop for an after-dinner treat. Better yet, he could make something specifically for the diner and you could offer it to the patrons for slightly more than you paid."

Nacho seemed to mull over the idea. "You know, that's not a bad plan at all. Everyone would benefit. The customers receive good food regardless of where they visit, and both of our businesses will thrive. The only question now is whether or not Señor Vela would be agreeable to it."

"There's only one way to find out."

Victoria snatched up her book from the place it still sat on the counter. She glanced over at her brother and nodded at the baby. "One can care for their family without sacrificing themselves in the process."

"I wish our parents had realized that," Lucas stated sadly.

"Let's prove we learned it for them," Victoria said. Then she left her brother to contend with his own battles while she saw to hers.

CHAPTER 9

*A*lejandro walked up to the counter and took a seat.

"I was wondering when you'd make yer way in here," the bartender welcomed him with an outstretched hand. "Name's Seamus Malone. Welcome to my saloon—soon to be one of the finest hotels and entertainment in these parts."

"Good to meet you," Alejandro said and shared his name with the man as well.

"So, what can I do ya for?"

"I'm throwing something of a celebration next week—a little something for the folks here in town—and I was hoping you might have a bit of rum. I was thinking it might give my confections a little kick for the few folks desiring something… extra."

"Rum, ya say? Now that is some fancy drinking there. I can check in the back, but I've got to tell you now that I highly doubt there'd be anything like that. Most of what I have is whiskey or rotgut."

Alejandro held back a grimace. Whiskey wouldn't taste very good in his confections and rotgut was something he wouldn't serve an enemy. There was no telling what was in that stuff. Alejandro had heard of places that cut their good whiskey with everything from turpentine to gunpowder, sometimes covering up the bitter taste with blackberry liquor or some sort of sweet juice to make it more palatable. This Seamus fellow didn't seem the sort to do such a thing, and it was possible he only added water to his so-called rotgut. Alejandro wasn't sure on any point. Still, it was a chance he wasn't sure he really wanted to take. Besides, whiskey of any sort wouldn't work for his plans anyway because it would fail to properly pull out the sugar in the recipe.

"I think I'll pass, but thank you all the same. If you get any in, keep me in mind. I like a nice rum now and then."

"Will do," Seamus said and bid him farewell.

There were still plenty of other things to do before the week was out, and he mentally listed them as he walked down the street, back towards his shop. Aside from the preparations for the *fiesta* itself, Alejandro and his sister were readily making arrangements for their mother's move ever since his aunt's correspondence had arrived two days earlier. The sanitarium he thought would keep his mother safe was found to be doing anything but that. When he read his aunt's letter sharing news about the terrible experiments taking place within its walls, it took everything in his power—as well as his levelheaded sister—to keep him from going there and razing the place with his bare hands. Thankfully, he had paid handsomely for his mother's care—which meant she had endured far less torture than many of the other residents. Still, to think that the possibility existed at all... Well, it was something he couldn't think about. At least, not now. Not in this moment and not until he saw his mother safely arrived and settled into a new, quieter life in Noelle.

The timing couldn't have been more perfect, either. He

was already planning a party. What more could he have to celebrate than his family being reunited?

A flash of a certain baking woman dressed in white—and not the kind that meant caked in flour from head to toe—played with his mind. He thought back to that evening he shared with Victoria. It wasn't so terribly long ago, and the hurt was still fresh. Despite what he told himself, he really did care about her. If he were to have ever settled down, she would have been the sort of woman he chose to share a future with.

That is, he *thought* she would have been the sort.

Alejandro pushed the thought aside with a sigh as he reached the store. He knew Julieta would be manning the front, so it would be safe to go in through the back—for both of them. In his surly mood, he didn't really feel much like seeing any customers. He stuck his key in the door and kicked the dust off his boots before entering the kitchen. The place looked the same as always and he ambled around until his eyes landed on the wood sign he and his sister had finished working on the day before. He held it up and admired the work, the chiseled wording of *"Cinco de Mayo"* in pretty script. The boards had been painted with the bit of whitewash leftover from when he painted the building, and Julieta had added a little flair to the sign with a garland of wild flowers she had picked.

"This will do nicely," his sister had said. He tried to argue with her that the flowers would wilt long before that coming Saturday, but she was not to be deterred. She had held her head up and explained, "I'll simply pick more."

He still wondered how "nicely" it all really was. Part of him didn't really feel like he had a right to be putting the sign up. When he first started, it was solely for the intent of finding a reason to throw a *fiesta* and Cinco de Mayo was the next one on the calendar. However, the more he worked at the small details, the more he realized a part of him was doing it *for* Victoria—not in spite of her. Every little thing he thought of—from food to decorations—always carried with it the curious wonder of whether or not she would appreciate the choice. Would she have approved?

Deciding to take the sign out front and hang it, he shook his head with irritation as he entered the main room, catching the sight of Julieta in the corner with a book in hand as she waited for a customer to make her selection. The color of her hair immediately reminded him of Victoria. He suppressed a growl. What was he to do? The woman had managed to really get under his skin... and the chime of the front bells confirmed his aching suspicion that she was there to stay, too. He hadn't even made it halfway into the shop and there she stood in the doorway, staring at him.

"In or out," he gruffly said. He softened a little at the sight of her wary expression, which she cast at the other lady in the shop. The customer quickly made her purchase and squeezed past Victoria, who still remained in the threshold. Alejandro lowered his voice. "I don't wish to fill the shop with flies."

Victoria quickly stepped through the entrance, shutting the door behind her. "Yes, that would make sense. I would think they like your chocolate as much as everyone else does."

"I'm not so sure that's entirely true. Business isn't exactly what I wanted it to be."

"Has it been bad?"

He frowned. "Is that what you've been hoping for?"

"Of course not. I just thought I might have a way to help make it better."

"Why? Are you feeling guilty for trying to steal away my customers?"

He noticed then that she carried a large book with her

when she shifted it under one arm, freeing the other so she could plant a fist on her hip. "I did no such thing, and you know it."

"Do I?" he challenged her and mimicked her actions by cradling the sign in one arm and making his own stand. "Then why did you use the box of chocolates I gave you for your cousin's diner? They were meant for your enjoyment. I didn't realize your idea of joy included drumming up more business."

Victoria huffed. "It wasn't me. Perhaps you would have known that sooner had you stayed and listened to what I had to say."

"Well, I'm listening now. If it wasn't you, then how do you explain it?"

"My brother woke in the morning and found them along with a few new recipes I wrote down in my book—recipes that had originally been meant for you."

"You created recipes for *me*?" The idea stirred something in him, but he quickly pushed it aside. "Never mind that. How is it possible you weren't aware of what he was doing? I could smell what he was baking as soon as the kitchen door swung open."

Alejandro didn't add the fact that it had been an incredible smell that made his mouth water for a taste.

"I wasn't even there. I was at the Golden Nugget."

His mouth dropped open with surprise. "What would you be doing in a place like that?"

She shrugged. "Simple enough. I needed a place to stay."

"Whatever for?" Alejandro asked. "I can't imagine your cousin putting you out."

"Of course not." Victoria briefly explained the evening's events after she and Alejandro parted. "So, you can see why I thought it best that I be the one to stay at the saloon. Lucas has suffered enough... I didn't want him tempted into nursing his hurt with more drink."

"I understand," Alejandro said. He was mildly grateful then that Seamus hadn't had any rum on hand. The cordials he wished to make didn't *really* need any alcohol in them—neither did the traditional cake he had wanted to try his hand at—not if it would mean Victoria's brother suffering trouble. It no longer disturbed him to know that her opinion of him mattered. Not after she explained everything that had happened. In fact, he felt something of a fool for having doubted her to begin with. He cleared his throat. "I—I think I owe you an apology."

"That's not necessary."

"Yes, it is. It was terribly wrong of me to accuse you of working against us. My sister told me there had to be a reasonable explanation." He glanced over to where Julieta pretended to busy herself, wiping down already clean countertops. She turned away, but not before Alejandro caught her smirk—a telltale sign that she would gloat over how she had been right all along whenever the moment to do so presented itself. He returned his attention to Victoria. "Do you think you can forgive me?"

"There is nothing to forgive."

"I'm not so sure about that." Alejandro pulled out the sign that he and his sister had worked so diligently on. "I stole your holiday."

"Stole my... Oh, I see. Such a funny way of putting it." She studied the sign for a moment. "Why did you think you should have a Cinco de Mayo celebration?"

"Honestly? The idea first began simply because I wanted to throw a party to attract more customers, and it was the next one on the calendar. However, I started liking the idea as our plans grew. I have never felt like I've won at anything. First, I lost my island, and in some strange sense, I then felt like I lost myself too. Then I lost my father, the best years of my childhood... the business I had hoped to open in Santa Sierra when the town missed out on the railroad. I'm even the cause of my mother losing her dignity, and the reason she's coming here. You can see why the holiday is an attractive one, can't you? A small town holding down their own with only a little help from the army, defeating invaders and saving not only their town, but their country? Well, that's impressive by any standards."

"I never really thought of it like that," she said. "I suppose that I, too, was caught up in all that I lost to really appreciate the significance of what it meant—the sacrifice that people like my parents made in order for others to go on. I thought that only someone who didn't care about their family would do something so foolish. Now I realize that people who love their family will protect them at all costs."

"Isn't that what you were doing for your brother—protecting him from what possible bad could happen?"

Victoria nodded. "Yes, I suppose I was doing the same for my cousin, too. I wanted to keep the peace and show my gratitude, thinking that working for him would do that."

"And sacrificing your own dreams all the while?"

She nodded again.

"So, what do you think you will do now?"

Before she could answer, the bells tinkled once more and another customer, her dress a drab, dark fabric with a matching shawl to cover her hanging head half hidden behind a mass of mousy hair, quietly entered. Alejandro motioned to the sign. "Let's take this outside."

Out front, Alejandro searched for a good spot. He immediately ruled out the window, once again cracked open so the sweet smells from his shop could float out into the streets, enticing customers to stop by. He finally chose a spot in front of the building, beside the door, and positioned the sign to lean against the whitewashed wood before turning back to Victoria.

"You never answered my question. Will you continue working for your cousin?"

"I suppose that depends on whether or not I have any other job offers."

He cracked a smile. "There's always me... I mean, us, here at the shop. You could always come work with us."

"Hey," a voice called from the window. "Is that the best you have to offer?"

"Josefina!" Victoria exclaimed. "I didn't even recognize you in that outfit."

Her cousin pulled the shawl and wig off. "That's because it's not mine. It belongs to your brother!"

"Her brother?" Alejandro looked confused. "Wait a minute. Are you saying *that* dress..."

Josefina nodded.

"And the wi—wig," Victoria sputtered. "But how is that possible?"

"Oh, you wouldn't believe it if I told you. It seems there is more to your brother than meets the eye... Perhaps the same could be said here?"

Victoria blushed. "What are you talking about?"

With a frustrated sigh, Josefina pulled the wig and shawl off. "Come now, *prima*. Let's not play games."

Another face popped into the window.

"She's right," Julieta admonished her brother. "I know you're braver than that."

Alejandro laughed. "The two of you remind me of the old women back home, who sit in their windows and yell down to the ones sitting on the stoops."

The women laughed.

"Do they really do that?" Victoria asked.

"Yes," Alejandro answered. "I remember old lady Sanchez

playing matchmaker from upstairs. Her son was courting a young woman and she yelled down to him, 'Kiss her, you fool.' I don't think any of us laughed so hard before."

Victoria laughed, but it was cut short by Julieta's demand.

"So when are *you* going to kiss her, you fool?"

"Julieta!" her brother admonished before turning to Victoria. "I'm so sorry. You'll have to forgive my little sister. Sometimes she gets wild thoughts."

"Oh, I don't mind." Victoria smiled sweetly. "It didn't seem so wild to me."

Alejandro's eyes grew wide. "You mean, after everything I've said and done—"

"I've already told you, Alejandro. All of that is in the past. What I'm interested in now is the future."

He glanced up at the two ladies who still studied them from the window, and then turned to Victoria to formally ask, "Would you care to take a walk with me and discuss this future you see?"

She took hold of his offered arm and they took a stroll down the street. "So, what is it you would like to know?"

"Tell me something about what you see for yourself."

She cocked her head, a dreamy look filling her eyes. "Well, I would still like to have my own little place—a spot where I can spend my days baking the most glorious bread imaginable."

"Done." Alejandro snapped the fingers of his free hand. "You can use the Vela kitchen to bake to your heart's content."

"You mean like partners?"

"Something like that."

Her eyes glossed over. "You would do that for me?"

Her tear-filled stare encouraged him to give her hand a light squeeze. "It's nothing really."

"It's something to me. In fact, it's like a dream come true."

His face looked thoughtful. "I hope it isn't—a dream come true, that is. Perhaps your dream could also include marriage... maybe even a family of your own one day?"

A smile stretched across her face. "Oh, yes. Those things would be nice to have, too." She bashfully glanced away. "Of course, there's always the matter of finding the right man who would want the same."

At the suggestion, he shamelessly drew her closer. "What if this man is nearer than you think?"

Her breath caught. "This seems awfully informal."

"You mean a bit like courting?"

Her cheeks warmed again. "Perhaps a little."

"Would that be such a bad thing?"

"No, not at all. To be honest, I think I would quite like that."

"It's kind of hard to court a woman properly, though. It's not like back east. There's so much to do out here—long hours at the shop. What if I wanted to find a little plot of land one day and build a house, too?"

"You mean like Nacho and Josefina?"

"That's right. There would be even more work involved then."

"I see what you mean. There wouldn't be much time for courting at all. Perhaps that's why people marry so fast out here."

Alejandro stopped and faced her. "Would that bother you much? To promise yourself to someone you've only known a month of Saturdays?"

"Has it been that long?" she coyly replied.

"This Saturday will make it one month that we've known one another... Wait a minute. You're playing with me."

She laughed. "Maybe a little."

"Then will you think about it? I mean, about my proposal."

"Mmm... the day of the Cinco de Mayo *fiesta*. Yes, knowing you for a month seems like a good reason to throw a party... and maybe we could have even more reason to celebrate. It seems as good a day as any to perform a wedding."

"Then you agree? I know I come emptyhanded at the moment, but I promise you'll be a partner in all that I have."

"Oh, Alejandro. I appreciate your offer and know you'll be good for it, but that isn't why I'll marry you. There's just something that feels right when I'm with you—like maybe the good Lord made something special just for me. What if this is my moment?"

He interlaced his fingers with her smaller ones. Then and wrapped the other arm loosely around her.

"Our moment," he said and placed the gentlest of kisses on her lips, releasing her before raising too many curious looks from passerby. "I will see you this Saturday."

"Yes," she said. "I'll come bearing baked goods and a crossdressing brother."

They both laughed.

"That's a story I can't wait to hear," he said.

EPILOGUE

*acho's Tacos*
Saturday, el 5 de Mayo

"Tighter," Victoria insisted and gripped the back of the bedpost as hard as she could.

Josefina gave another tug on the laces, but failed to draw the corset further in. "The only way it's getting any tighter is if you stop breathing."

"Oh, I knew I should have never sampled all those pastries. I only wanted to make sure Alejandro's mother was getting the very best when she arrived. Now my waistline is paying for it," Victoria lamented.

"Stop that. You know very well you've lost far too much weight this past month. Besides, I have it on good authority that 'you are a rare and natural beauty.'" A mischievous grin graced her cousin's face. "I heard Alejandro say as much last night."

"You were listening to our conversation!"

Josefina shrugged. "It's not my fault if the man speaks louder than everyone else."

Victoria giggled. "I think that's the way of his people—or perhaps simply how things are in the east. I don't know, but I like it. I think it makes him seem quite strong."

"Yes, I suppose it does. Although, I would dare say my Nacho is not one to be trifled with when it matters most. Yet, people are none the wiser because he quietly goes about his business."

"That's always been his way. Even as a child, he went about his business in a manner so that no one would notice him. Of course, that might have had something to do with the fact that his father wanted to raise a brood of cowboys... and Nacho only wanted to be a cook!"

"Much like your Alejandro—except he likes to make chocolate."

"They have a word for this, you know. My brother, Lucas, told me they call it a 'chocolatier.' It's French."

"To think of all your brother has seen and done. Well, it's no wonder he takes to the drink now and then. That's not to say I condone such behavior. I'm only stating that it would be difficult to live such a rambling, dangerous life."

"Yes," Victoria agreed, "it's no wonder he doesn't wish to settle down."

The women fell silent then and Josefina busied herself with pinning the last of Victoria's curls into place. She spun her cousin around to face the mirror.

"There you go. As beautiful as any bride should be on her wedding day."

Tears filled Victoria's eyes.

"Now, now." Josefina admonished her with a shake of one finger. "You better save that for after the vows, or your face will look a mess."

Victoria confidently nodded. Then a worried expression

marred her pretty features. "Do you think anyone will even come?"

"Do I think… Are you serious, *prima*? You must not know about all the food that's been arriving this morning."

"All the food?"

"Yes. Avis—you remember, the one married to the Liam— she brought by some of her best fried chicken just a while ago. She's not the only one, either. Many of the women I first rode out here with have done similar, bringing all sorts of goods to pitch in."

"You mean, none of them think it's strange that I'm marrying a man I only met a month ago?"

Josefina laughed. "We were mail order brides. Remember? Some of us married only a day or two after meeting our intendeds. Even Nacho and I married after only nine days. No, *prima*. Believe me when I say that no one thinks it strange at all. Besides, it shouldn't matter what others say— only how you feel about it." She looked at Victoria curiously. "How *do* you feel about it?"

"Oh, I don't know. Excited… nervous… I guess you could say I have all the feelings today."

"Sounds like a bride to me."

Victoria embraced her. "Thank you, Josefina, for all that you've done to help me get ready—and especially for loaning me the dress."

"You're welcome. Now, come. Let's get you out there so the party can begin."

Victoria led the way followed by Josefina, with both women being joined by Julieta as they made their way out of the small apartment Victoria had called her home for the past month. The women grabbed small bouquets of wild-flowers that Julieta had picked earlier that morning.

"They're beautiful," Victoria said when handed her bouquet. She inhaled deeply, all the while wondering how she could possibly use the flowers for a centerpiece on a cake one day.

Or perhaps some chocolate masterpiece?

She tucked the thought away as they passed through the kitchen and into the dining room. The tables, filled with incredible foods prepared or brought by family and friends, had been pushed to one side of the diner. The chairs were lined up in the remaining space, making two neat rows for the invited guests. As Nacho softly strummed on his guitar, Lucas joined Victoria.

"I suppose it's a good thing I stumbled into town," he quietly joked. "Now you'll have someone to give you away."

"You're not getting rid of me that easily," Victoria playfully whispered back. "You're not giving me away. You're gaining a brother."

Their lighthearted banter subsided as they approached the designated spot where Alejandro awaited, his mother sitting directly behind him in the front row. She smiled, making Victoria feel every bit like she had gained a mother as she did the day before when the older woman called her *"mi'ja."*

Nacho strummed the last chord as Victoria took her rightful place next to her intended.

"Dearly beloved," Reverend Chase began. Although, whatever else he said after that could hardly be recalled—despite the fact that Victoria somehow made it through her vows. The only thing she could recall were his last words.

"You may kiss the bride."

Alejandro did just that, leaving Victoria with a memory sweeter than all the chocolate covered churros the two would one day make together.

LETTER TO READERS

There's this movie with John Travolta called *Michael*. It's one of my favorites. Basically, it's about an angel who comes down to earth for one last hurrah. Since it's his final furlough from Heaven, he's enjoying all of life's "pleasures." However, he's also there to do battle. Whether that's challenging a bull grazing in a field or taking part of a bar fight, he's ready to face things head on. That also includes helping the man he helped "create" to get past his hang-ups and fall in love. Overall, it's a really good movie. It's not only uplifting (of course, there's a happily ever after). It's also inspiring.

In *Victoria ~ a Cinco de Mayo Bride*, there are many personal battles going on. Josefina and Nacho struggle to start a family of their own. Lucas, the heroine's brother, runs away from the family he's started as he battles the bottle. The hero, Alejandro, is something of an overachiever because he's lost so much in life. Then there's the heroine, Victoria, who suffers from low self-esteem despite the fact that she loves food and baking is a dream of hers. So, she begins to starve herself with the hope that she'll lose weight and become marriage material. Sadly, it takes the hero telling her that she's beautiful to help her get past that—sort of. In the end, concern about her weight is something that briefly pops up once more and her cousin has to remind her that she's fine the way she is.

See, that's the thing. Sometimes we can have all the best people telling us all the right things, but we'll still struggle to see the truth—the God-given beauty in ourselves. Now that's the bottom line. God doesn't make mistakes... and He made you. Right? That means you were made perfect and for a very specific purpose. It can be hard to see that at times, or to discern what your purpose may be, but it's so important that you know that you are beautiful and worthy and life-affirming in ways that you might not even know. Perhaps you're the one who smiles when a stranger walks by—and that smile was what they needed just to get through their day. Maybe (speaking from personal experience) you saw a single mom walking in the rain with her little ones, and you were the taxi driver who pulled over to offer a ride—free of charge.

Never forget. There is good in the world. You are that good.

Hmmm...

I wonder if Lucas can be the good that Greta needs.

Montana Sky Series

Friends of Noelle
Book One

Dust Bowl Desires

kindle worlds

MIMI MILAN

PROLOGUE

 *weetwater Springs, MT*
April 1877

"My, what a fortunate surname. *Gold.* Why, I bet your family is even blessed with such... Well, just look at you. I'm sure you could have played Goldilocks herself with those tresses."

Greta smiled at the elderly woman, glad that her decision to drop the "stein" from her last name had panned out. She may not have followed any particular religious beliefs, but that didn't mean she wasn't still Jewish by blood—a fact that most individuals in the area didn't care for. "Thank you, ma'am. That's a fairytale favorite of mine."

"I'm sure it is." The woman nodded. "Now tell me, Mrs. Gold—"

"Oh, it's just Miss—not Missus."

"I beg your pardon?"

Greta hesitated. "I—That is to say, I'm not married. I'm simply Miss Gold."

The woman looked pointedly at the one month old infant

Greta cradled and then back at the young woman. "But you have a baby."

"Yes, ma'am. That's right."

The woman continued to stare at her. After what seemed like many long moments, she sniffed quite loudly. Then she abruptly stood and crossed the receiving room to the front door. She unceremoniously opened it. "I'm sorry you've traveled all this way for nothing, *Miss* Gold. However, I have no rooms to rent at the moment."

Greta haltingly followed the woman. She stopped in the threshold only to make one last plea, her voice filled with distress. "Please, ma'am. I don't think you understand. I really have nowhere else in the world to go, and there's this wee one to worry for as well. Please let us stay. I can cook for you. I clean, too. I promise you'll not find another who works as hard as I."

Her voice had grown several decimals louder, alerting the child to trouble. At the sound of her dismay, the baby opened his mouth wide and wailed a glorious, ear piercing cry.

Greta jostled the baby, anxiously trying to calm him. "He won't make a sound. I promise. He'll be like an angel."

The woman only held the door wider.

"Listen, girl. I run a clean house." She glared at Greta. "Besides, you can't produce an angel out of the Devil's doing. Now, get out of my home."

The women stared at one another for several more seconds. Then, with feet as heavy as cold lead, Greta stumbled out onto the front porch and back down to where she had parked her wagon. Balancing the baby in one arm, she hiked her skirts up as high as she dared—part of her fearing the old woman still watched, and the other part wishing the lady be damned to the very place she had dared indicate Greta's child hailed from.

"The nerve of that wicked wretch," she quietly seethed

under her breath as she settled into the wagon and placed her son in the cradle of blankets she had constructed for him, several stacks of books—her only valuable possessions aside from her child—arranged all around him like mini, protective walls. Back in his safe resting space, the baby finally quieted. "That's right, my boy. We neither want nor need that horrible woman. Devil, indeed."

She picked up the leather leads and gave them a snap, setting the horses in motion, all the while knowing that it was for the best things didn't work out with Old Lady Hobble—as so many others in Sweetwater Springs had come to call her. To think the woman who seemed so sweet whenever they passed one another in the mercantile or church could have such a sharp tongue...

Isn't there a scripture for that, Greta wondered but for a moment. It had been too many years since she had read the Tanakh, and she had never read a Christian's bible. Besides, she didn't want to think too deeply on it. Doing so would mean she had to think about her own sin and, for as much as she hated to admit it, what she and Lucas did together had been just that. Still, it was only one moment of bad judgment and she couldn't think that such a blessing as her sweet babe could be a curse. All children were heavenly blessings.

What she needed to do was convince Lucas of that. If she could, then maybe they would marry. If they were married, then her son would be legitimate. If her son was legitimate...

She could finally return home.

CLICK HERE TO CONTINUE READING.

ABOUT THE AUTHOR

Mimi Milan is an award winning, bestselling Latin American poet and author of both historical and contemporary fiction. The majority of her stories feature characters who resemble the melting pot of people she grew up with (from New Jersey to Mexico), as well as the languages she speaks (English, Spanish, and Italian).

A candidate for the MFA in Creative Writing at Queens University, Mimi is thrilled to live the dream of playing with imaginary friends every day.

She thanks you for the support you've shown her and invites you to follow her on Amazon or connect online:

www.mimimilan.com
https://www.bookbub.com/profile/mimi-milan
www.facebook.com/AuthorMimiMilan
www.twitter.com/thewritingMimi
http://writemimimilan@gmail.com